THE YOUNG CITY

THE UNWRITTEN BOOKS

THE
YOUNG CITY

James Bow

DUNDURN PRESS
TORONTO

Editor: Barry Jowett
Design: Jennifer Scott
Printer: Webcom

Library and Archives Canada Cataloguing in Publication

Bow, James, 1972-
    The young city : the unwritten books / by James Bow.

ISBN 978-1-55002-846-1

    I. Title.

PS8603.O973Y69 2008   jC813'.6   C2008-906212-4

1   2   3   4   5   12   11   10   09   08

Canada   Conseil des Arts du Canada   Canada Council for the Arts   ONTARIO ARTS COUNCIL / CONSEIL DES ARTS DE L'ONTARIO

We acknowledge the support of **The Canada Council for the Arts** and the **Ontario Arts Council** for our publishing program. We also acknowledge the financial support of the **Government of Canada** through the **Book Publishing Industry Development Program** and **The Association for the Export of Canadian Books**, and the **Government of Ontario** through the **Ontario Book Publishers Tax Credit** program, and the **Ontario Media Development Corporation**.

Care has been taken to trace the ownership of copyright material used in this book. The author and the publisher welcome any information enabling them to rectify any references or credits in subsequent editions.

                                                        J. Kirk Howard, President

Printed and bound in Canada.
Printed on recycled paper.

www.dundurn.com

Dundurn Press	Gazelle Book Services Limited	Dundurn Press
3 Church Street, Suite 500	White Cross Mills	2250 Military Road
Toronto, Ontario, Canada	High Town, Lancaster, England	Tonawanda, NY
M5E 1M2	LA1 4XS	U.S.A. 14150

~~ :•: ~~

For Nora

~~ :•: ~~

Chapter One

~~ :•: ~~

UNDERCURRENTS

Peter McAllister kicked open the door and tottered down the basement steps, looking like a box with legs. "Box of books," he puffed. "Again. Where do these go?"

Rosemary Watson dropped the roll of carpet and rubbed her hands against her jeans. Her halter top was smudged with dirt. She peered around at the whitewashed brick and the concrete floor and pushed her glasses further up on her nose. "Theo, you're paying *how* much to rent this place?"

Her brother, Theo, smiled ruefully. "Seven hundred dollars a month. Plus utilities."

"For this dungeon?"

Peter swayed. "Box. Books. Where do they go?"

"Location, location, location," said Theo. "For seven hundred dollars I could get a wonderful place ... an hour away. I don't need anything fancy. With my doctoral work, I'll probably just be here to sleep."

"Books!" yelled Peter.

"Well, the outside is nice," said Rosemary. "Gingerbread, pocket garden, nice old Victorian. I can't believe we're in downtown Toronto. But I'm sure the original builders didn't intend to have you living in the basement."

"Right, that's it!" said Peter. "I'm dropping these!"

Theo and Rosemary grabbed the box from Peter's hands. He sagged into a chair, fanning himself with a discarded scrap of cardboard. "Why does it always have to be a hot day when people move?"

"Poor Peter!" Rosemary stepped behind him and wrapped him in a hug. "And we're only just starting out. Then it's up to Waterloo to move me into my dorm, and then over to London to move you into your apartment."

"Don't remind me," Peter huffed. He clasped and kissed her hands.

"Looking forward to university, you two?" asked Theo.

"Yeah!" said Peter. "Welcome to adulthood!"

Rosemary took a deep breath. "Welcome to rent."

"Welcome to no curfew," said Peter.

"Grocery bills."

"Privacy!"

"Roommates."

Peter chuckled. "Don't be a killjoy."

She slapped his hair. "I am not a killjoy!"

"A worrywart, then." He caught her wrist and kissed it.

She giggled. "I'm practical!" She bent toward him and they shared a kiss.

Theo rolled his eyes. "You two are shameless."

Rosemary pulled away briefly and gave her brother a sly grin. "Us? Shameless?"

"No idea what you're talking about," added Peter when he was able.

Theo sighed. "Here!" He thrust one box at Peter and another at Rosemary. "Take these into the bedroom and straighten up in there. I'll make some lemonade."

Peter and Rosemary dutifully carried their boxes into the back room. Other boxes were already stacked up in all corners, and bits of a futon were piled by one wall.

Peter set about rearranging some piles. Then he turned and walked straight into Rosemary, who put her arms around him and gave him a kiss that left him short of breath.

"Rosemary," he whispered. He cleared his throat. "We're in Theo's apartment."

"Yes," she said, with a wild tinge to her smile. "His nice, quiet, private apartment."

He coughed. "Yes," he said. "*Theo's* apartment. Which you called a dungeon."

"It's a private dungeon."

"Rosemary, he's in the next room."

"We could send Theo out to pick up pizzas or something. Tell him we'll put together some furniture and, when he's gone, kiss and ... stuff."

Peter's eyebrows went up. "Won't Theo be suspicious if nothing gets put together?"

"We could put his futon together and ... make use of it."

He blanched and swallowed. "What's gotten into you?"

She giggled and pressed close. "Just teasing Theo.... A little," she whispered. "Showing him his little sister isn't so little anymore."

Peter scowled. "*Just* teasing?"

"Not just, silly!"

Peter grinned. Their lips met.

At the door, Theo cleared his throat. He stood, frowning at them, holding a tray with a pitcher of lemonade and three glasses. Peter jumped back so fast Rosemary staggered. She shot Peter a glare, then took the tray and poured out the lemonade. The three of them stood in the middle of Theo's bedroom, drinking silently.

Finally, Theo set his drink aside. "Rosemary, could I ask you something?"

"Shoot," she said as Peter took another swig of his lemonade.

"Are you and Peter having sex?" asked Theo.

Peter choked on his lemonade.

"Theo!" Rosemary stared at her brother in open-mouthed shock. "How dare you?"

"You have your hands on Peter right in front of me, and you ask how dare *me*?"

Gagging, coughing, Peter barely managed to set his glass down on top of a stack of boxes. He leaned against the wall, clutching his chest.

Rosemary spluttered. "It's none of your business."

"Rosemary, you're my little sister," said Theo. "I need to know you're being careful."

"I don't need to tell you about my love life," Rosemary snapped.

"So you *have* been having sex," said Theo.

"I didn't say that!" shouted Rosemary.

Peter took deep breaths of air. He doubled over and began coughing again.

"Look, it's a simple question," Theo began.

"It's a huge question!" yelled Rosemary. "You're not my dad."

"I'm your brother."

"That's not the same thing!"

"Look, you've been getting pretty serious," said Theo. "I mean, you two have been serious for years, but there's serious, and then there's *serious*. Where did you two go after the prom?"

Rosemary reddened. "Nowhere — I mean, around."

"Rosemary ..."

"Look, Mom and Dad didn't complain," said Rosemary. "So we were a couple of hours late. No big!

I called them and told them, and they said we could stay out a bit later. If they had a problem with what we were doing, they would have told me."

"Your parents think the world of you and trust you to make your own decisions," said Theo. "But they're in their fifties, and I'm twenty-four. I have a better memory of what kids your age get up to."

"So, why were *you* two hours late coming back after *your* prom?" asked Rosemary.

"None of your business."

"Aha!"

"Aha!" Theo shot back.

Rosemary reddened and clenched her fists.

Wheezing, thumping his chest, Peter got his breath back. "Theo," he gasped. "Rosemary and I, we —"

"Don't answer him," snapped Rosemary. "It doesn't matter if we do or not. We're mature enough to decide —"

"You're *not* mature," said Theo. "Not really. And I don't mean that in a bad way, either. You're both barely out of high school, and yet I hear you two talking about marriage."

Peter goggled. Rosemary blanched. "You've been eavesdropping?"

"Look, just don't rush into things," said Theo, raising his hands. "Take it from somebody who knows. University is not high school, and undergraduate university is not like graduate studies. You think you know where you stand? Well your world is going to change. Be careful."

Rosemary looked at him, hurt. "You don't think we'd be careful?"

Theo sighed. "Look, I'm sorry. It's just that ... Just humour your older brother, okay? I don't want you to have any regrets."

Rosemary rolled her eyes. "Okay," she said at last. "I promise. We'll be careful."

"That's my Sage," said Theo. He opened his arms.

She made a face at his use of her long-abandoned nickname, but she came forward and hugged him.

"And you didn't answer my question," said Theo.

"And I'm not going to," said Rosemary, her voice muffled by his chest.

Theo shrugged. "All right. Well, how about I go and get us a pizza ...," he said, flashing them a smile and then adding, "... by calling and having it delivered. The phone's set up, so I don't have to leave you two alone for long." He grinned at their reddened cheeks and left the room.

When Theo was gone, Peter rounded on Rosemary. "Why didn't you just tell him 'no'? It would have been so much easier."

She glared. "It's not his business."

Peter huffed and turned away. They went back to cleaning up the room in silence. Then, as Peter picked up a tossed-aside throw rug, something caught his attention and he knelt on the bare concrete. When Theo entered the room, Peter asked, "Theo, did you know you have a hole in your floor?"

Theo and Rosemary turned. The three of them crouched by an opening in the concrete the size of a quarter. Rosemary pulled a penny from her pocket and dropped it in the hole. It vanished without a sound. She tapped the floor. "It sounds hollow."

Peter slid back to the wall. "Seven hundred dollars a month?"

Theo nodded. "Plus utilities."

Rosemary peered into the hole. "Where do you think it goes?"

Theo stood and tapped the floor one foot from the hole, then three feet, then five. It rang hollow each time. He shrugged. "A cavern, maybe?"

Rosemary shot up. "Cavern?"

"Sure, there are supposed to be a few in the area. Taddle Creek used to flow through here until the city turned it into a storm sewer. I heard the river ran through caves. Maybe this is one of them."

Rosemary slid away from the hole.

Theo chuckled. "Oh, don't be a baby, Rosie. If it were really so unsafe, could I do this?" He began to jump around the hole in a violent dance.

Rosemary pressed her back to the wall. "Theo!"

Theo laughed. "Sorry, Rosie. Now, if we're done teasing each other ..."

In the kitchen, the phone rang.

Theo turned. "That's probably the pizza place. They said they'd call to confirm the address because I'm a new customer. Wait here, you two." He left, leaving the two pressed against opposite walls.

Rosemary and Peter watched him go. Then, gingerly, they stepped forward and approached the hole. Peter tapped the concrete again, marvelling at the hollow sound it made.

"You ever hear of this Taddle Creek?" asked Rosemary.

Peter shook his head. "I only lived in downtown Toronto until I was ten. Wasn't exactly interested in urban archaeology."

"I wonder what's down there." Rosemary gave the floor her own experimental tap.

Cracks fissured from the hole and passed beneath their feet.

Peter and Rosemary flashed each other looks of horror.

The floor gave way. They fell into darkness.

~~ :•: ~~

Rosemary hit stone — hard. The impact winded her and kept her from catching herself before she rolled over an edge. There was another heart-stopping moment of freefall, and then she hit bottom with a splash.

Submerged, she clawed for the surface, choking on gritty, brackish water. She burst into air alive with the roar of a rushing stream.

"Peter!" she screamed. "Pete—." She slipped beneath the surface.

Hands clutched at her and hauled her up.

"Rosemary!" Peter shouted in her ear. "Are you all right?"

"Where are we?" She kicked against the current, catching his legs twice.

"Water! Stream! Grab something!"

"I'm trying!" She glubbed water again.

Then her shoulder smacked something sharp. Her hands clawed brick. Soon they were clinging to a wall, heads barely above water, bracing each other against the rushing stream.

"What now?" shouted Rosemary.

"We've got to get out of this water!"

"It's too dark!"

"Feel for a ledge! Anything! I'm slipping!"

Rosemary ran her hands over the wall. Above her head, she felt a shelf extending away, deep enough to lie on. She hauled herself up and rolled onto dry soil.

Turning on her stomach, she reached blindly for Peter, slapping him across the face before catching his wrist. He clutched her arm and, after a brief struggle, lay gasping beside her.

"Thank you," he wheezed.

She clasped him close. "Where are we?" she shouted in his ear.

He coughed. "I don't know. But this place stinks."

Now that they were out of danger, she could register what her other senses told her. The water drowned out all sound. The air was cool, damp, and foul. "Oh God, I hope we didn't fall into the sewer."

Peter sniffed his sodden sleeve. "No. We smell pretty bad, but not *that* bad."

"Storm sewer, then." Rosemary let out a hollow laugh. "Lucky us."

"How do we get out of here?" he gasped.

"Theo will help us."

"The stream pulled us quite a way," yelled Peter.

"We head back," said Rosemary. "We follow this ledge upstream."

They stood up, clutching each other, expecting to hit their heads on the ceiling. They found they could stand without stooping. There was no wall within arm's reach.

The storm sewer was a presence of sound and wind on their left. Save for the sandy ground beneath their feet, or the brick lip of the sewer if they ventured too far, they might as well have been wandering in a void. After what seemed like hours, Rosemary brushed stone on her right. "No!" she moaned. "It's closing in on us."

"Rosemary, wait! I can see you!"

She looked toward his voice and realized that she

could see him, too. He was a silhouette against shadow. "The hole must be nearby! We must be getting light from Theo's apartment!"

Peter shouted to the ceiling. "Theo! We're down here!"

Rosemary joined in. "Theo! Help! Get us out!"

Their words rang back at them, accompanied only by the roar of rushing water.

"Theo!" Rosemary screamed.

"Maybe he's gone for help," said Peter.

"Maybe ..."

"Where else could he be?" he said. "If he wasn't calling the fire department, he'd be sticking his head in the hole and shouting."

"You're right." She took a deep breath. "We should wait. That's sensible. Let's sit down." She slumped onto the sandy ground.

He knelt beside her. "You all right? You're shivering."

"So are you!"

"Not as bad as you. Here, let me hold you."

"I'm okay." But she leaned into his embrace.

They waited, breathing the damp, reeking air. Nobody called. Their clothes started to dry.

Rosemary pulled away from Peter and stood up. She couldn't pace, so she shifted on her feet, muttering, "Where is he? He should be back by now." She kicked the sand. "Theo!"

Peter grabbed her. "Rosemary, don't panic."

She slapped his hands away. "Don't you tell me not to panic! We're stuck here! I hate places like this!"

He shook her by the shoulders. "Rosemary!"

She stared at him, breathing heavily. "I'm sorry," she said at last. "I'm feeling a little claustrophobic. We have to get out of here."

"And go where?"

"Upstream. This water has to come from somewhere."

"Shouldn't we just —"

"Peter, do you really want to sit in the dark with Miss Claustrophobia for who knows how long?"

He took her hand. "Let's go."

Feeling along the sloping cavern wall beside them, they made their way upstream faster than before. Then, instead of touching sand, Peter's feet met brick, while Rosemary's met open air. She stumbled, slipped from Peter's grip, and fell with a splash.

"Rosemary!"

She picked herself up, rubbing her barked palms. "I'm okay," she shouted, stopping Peter from jumping in after her. "Just a little winded, that's all. And standing in this stupid sewer again."

"Let me help you out!" He scrambled for the edge.

"Wait, something's different." She peered around in the gloom. "I'm standing in this water. It's barely knee deep!" She stood in the centre of the stream and held out both arms. A step to her left and another to her right allowed her to touch slimy bricks on either side. "It's narrower. Round, too, like a pipe."

"Where did all that extra water come from?"

"I'll check." Holding on to the side, she crept forward. The roar was as loud as ever but, as she listened, it seemed to intensify in front of her. Then the wall turned sharply away and the floor deepened. The current tugged her sideways.

"It's a junction!" She struggled back. "The river branches! I'm standing in a smaller stream!"

"Can you come out now?"

"No, come in with me!"

"Are you nuts?"

"Look, a smaller stream means we're closer to the source — closer to an exit!" She glared at his silhouette. "We have to try! Take my hands."

Catching her hands, he jumped in. "I hope you're right."

"So do I."

Hand in hand, they sloshed upstream. The walls of the cavern converged above them. The pipe walls wrapped over them. Their splashes echoed. Peter reached for a ceiling and found it by standing on tiptoe.

"How's the claustrophobia?" he asked.

"Chugging merrily along."

They sloshed forward, stopping occasionally for Peter to reach up and check for manhole shafts and other ways out. Then, as they felt the pipe curving before them,

Rosemary whirled around. "What was that?"

"What?"

"That splashing sound."

"Probably water."

She smacked his shoulder. "Quiet! There it is again."

"Rosemary, don't spook yourself."

"I swear, something's following us!"

"Like what?" he snorted. "Crocodiles?" Then he heard it, too: a squeal, amplified by the pipe, then a sound like a stone thrown into a lake. "Okay ... Maybe a rat, but that's nothing to be alarmed about."

There were more echoing squeals. Then came a sound like a river reversing its flow. They became aware of a phosphor glow. Had it always been there, or was it creeping up the tunnel after them? Waves lapped at their knees.

In the growing light, Peter and Rosemary glanced at each other, turned, and struggled upstream.

As they stumbled and splashed, they saw a new light grow ahead of them, warm and yellow. They rushed forward, rounded a turn, and were suddenly outside. Sunlight sent them staggering, hands over their eyes, back toward the exit they'd emerged from. They leaned on a brick wall, the supernatural glow all but forgotten, taking deep gulps of the sweet air.

"I never knew Toronto air could smell this good," wheezed Rosemary.

Peter climbed over the wall and helped her onto a

muddy slope. They flopped onto their backs and stared at the sky.

They had emerged from a round, brick culvert, tall as a door. Its metal gate lay on the opposite embankment. The ditch snaked away, built of newer bricks, and square. The sky above them was blue and grey, with black clouds rolling away. The air smelled of rain. "No wonder the water was so rough," said Rosemary. "We had a summer thunderstorm."

"Hmm?" He looked up. "Rosemary, after all that, how can you still have your glasses?"

"Sports strap." She fingered a black elastic band stretching behind her ear and beneath her hair. "Perfect for my active lifestyle." Then she looked down. "Oh my! Look at us."

They were grey with mud, their clothes matted and clinging, their hair a disaster. Both carried the distinctive odour of the sewer.

Peter chuckled. "Theo's shower is going to get quite a workout."

"Shower? This dirt needs at least an hour's soak in the tub!"

"Oh, no!" said Peter. "You're not hogging the tub while I stink up Theo's apartment! I'll wrestle you for it!"

Rosemary giggled. "Maybe we can share."

He blinked at her. "You sure like teasing your brother."

"First time I've had ammunition."

He laughed and squeezed her hand. "I love you, Rosemary."

She squeezed back, and then they stared at each other, true relief sinking in. They embraced, and held on tight.

"I love you too," said Rosemary. She kissed his matted hair, then wrinkled her nose at the smell. She patted his shoulder. "Let's find out where we are."

They got to their feet. Peter peered over the rim of the embankment. "It's probably the university. Theo's apartment is just south of it."

"It's awfully quiet." Rosemary trudged up the slope.

Peter nodded to a stone building, all turrets and pointed windows, facing onto a large green. "It's the university, all right. I think that's King's College."

But Rosemary was looking back across the culvert. She'd turned pale. "Peter?"

"What's wrong?"

She pointed. "The city's gone."

He whirled around. "What?"

"The buildings have disappeared! It's all gone! Peter, what happened to Toronto?"

CHAPTER TWO

~~ :•: ~~

THE YOUNG CITY

P eter looked from Rosemary to the horizon and back again. "It couldn't have."

"It has!" Rosemary jumped to see if her view wasn't blocked by some rise. "Where's the CN Tower? Where are the skyscrapers?" She turned and stared at the turreted building across its wide green. "Peter, if this is the university, half of the buildings are missing!" She stared at Peter in horror.

He raised his hands. "No. There has to be some mistake. Maybe we got turned around. Maybe ...." He stopped and stared. Across a dying wetland, he *could* see a city: of gingerbread houses and church spires, like an old postcard or a hand-tinted photograph.

He stumbled back. Rosemary caught him.

"Who's there?"

The bellowing voice made them dive for cover. As they peered over the rim of the muddy embankment,

Rosemary noticed that they were in the middle of a deserted construction site. Large timbers were piled by huge stones and mounds of moved earth. A temporary wooden wall, made of planks, not plywood, hoarded everything inside.

Standing in the middle was a tall, stout man. Though stooped by time, he looked wary and dangerous as a wolf. He had a grizzled beard and fierce eyes. He held a plank like a club.

"Who's there?" he shouted again. "Thieves? Vandals? If I catch you, you'll regret it, you young ruffians!" He stalked toward the back of the site, crouching low.

"Where do we go?" whispered Peter.

"The front gate's open." She gripped his hand. "Let's go!"

They charged over the embankment and ran for the gate.

"There you are!" They heard the thump and splash of the watchman in pursuit. He clambered over a pile of timbers and leapt into their path, arms raised and ready to fight. His eyes widened at the sight of Rosemary in her jeans and muddy halter top. "A w-woman?"

She ploughed into him, sprawling him in the mud. Peter ducked around him. The watchman struggled to his feet and followed, but only to the gate. Peter and Rosemary kept running until his shouts faded in the distance. Then they stopped and caught their breath.

"You okay?" Peter gasped.

"Yeah," Rosemary wheezed. "Did you see the clothes he was wearing?" She stopped short. "We're standing on a wooden sidewalk ... by a dirt road. What *is* this, the wild west?"

The narrow, gabled row houses loomed on either side of them. The silence echoed. Peter shivered. "I don't think we're in Toronto anymore."

Then bells started ringing.

They peeled in all directions, shattering the silence, echoing off of brick and hill. Down the street, a squat church opened its Gothic doors and people streamed out. Men put on hats, women gathered up handfuls of skirts to descend the steps.

Rosemary fingered the tie of her halter top. The breeze chilled her bare back. Without a word, they turned and walked away as quickly as they could.

The bells stopped ringing, their echoes replaced by the new sounds of the city. Carriages rattled after hoofbeats, splashing and sucking the muddy roads. Hard soles clopped on the wooden sidewalks as crowds thronged like another form of rush hour. There was flannel and taffeta everywhere, lace and gingham. The underdressed teenagers hunched forward, willing themselves invisible. It didn't work.

Behind them, an old lady cried out, "Oh my goodness, that girl is naked!"

Rosemary flushed.

Heads turned. People stared.

"Vagrants!" somebody else called. "Street urchins!"

"They're filthy!"

Peter took a deep breath. "We'd better get off this street." He stepped off the sidewalk.

"Peter, look out!"

Horses whinnied and veered. Peter staggered back, but the wheel of a passing carriage clipped his leg and sent him sprawling. He hit his head on the wooden sidewalk and lay dazed.

"Peter!" Rosemary knelt by him. "Are you ..."

He moaned and rubbed his head. "I don't believe it. Never been hit by a car in my life, but the first horse and buggy comes along and whammo!"

Rosemary laughed nervously.

"Are you hurt?"

A young woman knelt beside them, her dark hair drawn back in a severe bun, but her face open and warm. She wore a plain cotton dress that didn't match her finer hat and gloves. She pulled Peter into a sitting position and gave his head a quick but thorough glance. "You are not bleeding." She touched the back of his head and he let out a yowl. "But you are going to have a bump, I'm afraid. How do you feel?"

"Okay, I guess." He winced. "A little stunned."

"Are you dizzy?" asked Rosemary. "How many fingers am I holding up?"

"Two," said Peter.

The woman gave Rosemary a sharp glance, but

returned her attention to Peter. "No, do not stand up yet. Get your breath back into you, first."

The crowd gave Peter and Rosemary a wide berth, creating a bottleneck on the sidewalk.

"Why don't you leave those two alone?" snapped a man in fine clothes. "They should have been watching where they were going!"

The woman's nostrils flared. "'Whatsoever you do unto the least of my people, you do unto me!' Did you not pay attention to today's sermon?" The man dismissed her with a wave of his hand.

As she turned back to Peter and helped him stand, she added, "You *should* have watched where you were going. You walked right into that carriage's path!"

"We'll be more careful next time," said Rosemary. "Thank you for helping us."

"You are most welcome. My name is Faith —"

"Get a move on!" shouted a man with a tall black hat. "We don't want your kind around here!"

"Scandalous that a woman should be seen like that in public!" said a middle-aged woman. "And on the Lord's Day, too!"

"I've a good mind to call the constabulary!"

Rosemary flinched. The last thing they needed right now was police.

Faith glared at the crowd. "Is this how you would treat people in need? What does it say about us that we should live so prosperously while such poverty exists?"

Peter leaned toward Rosemary. "What's with this woman's accent? She sounds almost British. Everybody sounds British."

Rosemary gripped his hand. A crowd had gathered, staring in bemusement at the underdressed couple and the dark-haired young woman who railed at passersby.

Then came the sound of running feet. "Police! Let us through!" The crowd parted, and two policemen strode in.

They wore dark blue coats with brass buttons, and bobby hats instead of caps. They smacked truncheons on their palms. Neither looked in the mood for a long explanation.

Rosemary tightened her grip on Peter's hand. "Let's get out of here!"

He stared at the constables. Faith was already remonstrating with them. "Run? But —"

Rosemary yanked him across the street.

"Hey! Stop!" The policeman brushed past Faith, leaving her staring after the couple, hands on her hips.

Rosemary and Peter slogged between horse and carriage, and then jumped onto the other sidewalk. They darted between people too startled to stop them, but the policemen, blowing their whistles with every breath, were hot on their trail.

"We have to hide!" Rosemary puffed.

"Where?"

They splashed across another muddy street and onto another wooden sidewalk. The crowds started to thin out, leaving the constables a clear line to follow them.

"Alleyway," Rosemary gasped.

They turned a corner, and were on a street lined with stores. The crowds were all but gone now, and all the stores were closed. There was a sign at the corner, fixed to one of the buildings. Peter stopped and stared.

"Yonge Street?" he exclaimed. "But it can't —"

Rosemary yanked him back into a run. "Come *on!*"

They dashed across the street, jumping over two sets of tracks running up the middle. They leapt across the sidewalk and into the sanctuary between two brick buildings.

The alley smelled of wet brick and rot. The walls towered two storeys above them and stretched to the next street. The nearest cover was a dark doorway, hidden by a pile of abandoned crates. They knelt on the drenched stones and held their breath.

They heard the approaching swift footfalls, hard soles on wood. There was a blur of blue past the alleyway, then the footfalls faded into the distance.

When silence came, Rosemary flopped onto the doorstep. "Okay, take stock. Where are we?"

Peter sat beside her. "Well, we fall down a hole, trek through an underground tunnel, and come out into this crazy place. Did you pass any rabbits running late?"

Rosemary let out a terse laugh. "We didn't walk too far, so we're still in Toronto. We shouldn't be too far from Theo's apartment, in fact."

Peter took a deep breath. "We've run for blocks. Theo's apartment was right downtown. We should have seen the skyline by now."

"Where do you think we are?"

He shrugged, but didn't meet her eye. "I just passed a sign that said Yonge Street."

"So?"

"I know Yonge Street. It's the main street of Toronto. It doesn't look a thing like this."

"Peter ..."

"What if the reason we haven't seen the skyline is because it hasn't been built ... yet?"

She stared at him. "No way. It's not time travel. That's impossible."

Peter reached behind the crates and smoothed out a wet and crumpled sheet of newsprint. He pointed to the banner. "*The Globe*. August 28, 1884. What do you say to that?"

"That paper can't be from 1884! It hasn't yellowed —"

"It wouldn't have yellowed if we were really in 1884 now, would it?"

She glared at him. "It's *not* time travel!"

He sighed. "Okay. Alternative theories: A historical film shoot."

Rosemary clapped her hands. "That's it! That would explain the clothes!"

"And why half the city is missing."

Rosemary drooped.

He looked at her slumped shoulders. "We *could* be inside a studio, I suppose," he offered.

Rosemary looked at the sky. "If so, that's one heck of a matte painting." She hugged her knees. "It's not a studio, is it?"

"No."

"Oh God, Peter. What are we going to do?"

"We'll go back," said Peter.

"How? The police are looking for us, we stick out like sore thumbs, and we just about got stoned to death!"

"We'll sneak back," said Peter. "We'll wait for night."

"It's going to get cold! It wasn't nearly this cold back at Theo's place! We're going to need ropes and ... and flashlights!"

"I got bad news for you there."

She thumped his shoulder. "Be serious! What are we going to do?"

"Well ..." He pursed his lips. "It's going to take time."

She stared at him. "We can't stay here. Theo would go out of his mind!"

"I don't think Theo knows we've gone yet."

She blinked. He went on. "Think about it. We were in that cavern for how long? Thirty minutes? Long enough for

Theo to notice we were gone. But if we've fallen through a time portal, then the rules are all out the window. Maybe only a second has passed on Theo's side. Theo may not even have heard the fall yet."

"You mean, we're on our own." Her voice was very small. She shivered. Peter reached out and held her close. She clung to him, and pressed her face into his shoulder. After a moment she pushed him away, clearing her nose with a sniff. "So, we're on our own. Fine. Let's get to work. We need lights. Torches or something. And climbing equipment."

Peter drew himself up. "We'll need food, first," he said. "And shelter. And new clothes. And a bath. We aren't going to get very far looking the way we do."

"So, we find work."

He frowned. "How are we going to find work looking like we've rolled on these streets?"

"Then the first thing we do is beg for clothes, or beg for money to buy clothes."

"Right," he said. "You lead the way."

They crept to the end of the alleyway and peered out at the stores. The mud-and-plank street stretched away on either side of them, with two tracks in the middle but no streetcars in sight. No overhead wires, either. Shops lined the sidewalks, their display windows dark and curtained.

"Yonge Street, huh?" Rosemary shook her head in disbelief.

"That's what the sign said."

"But nothing's open."

"'Course not," said Peter. "It's Sunday."

She glanced at him, so he explained. "Sunday shopping laws? The last ones weren't repealed until the early nineties. *Our* nineties. They get a lot stricter the further you go back."

Rosemary shook her head. "I leave Clarksbury to go to the big city and I end up in Clarksbury Senior." She sighed. "Why do these things happen to us?" She couldn't keep the whine out of her voice. She looked at him.

He thought a long moment, then shrugged. He held out his hands, palms up.

"But I blame you," he said.

She glared at him, then her frown eased when she saw his grin. She looked back south and pointed. "That store's open."

A grey-suited man, swinging his cane, walked up the plank sidewalk. He doffed his hat as he stepped into the doorway of a shop in the middle of a row of buildings.

Peter shrugged. "Proprietor? Some owners lived above their stores."

Then came the sound of a cane rapping against a door.

"The owner wouldn't knock." She stepped onto the sidewalk.

Before she'd taken two steps, Peter pulled her into the shadow of another doorway. He pointed.

Following the well-dressed man, a group of four boys in their mid-teens, wearing caps and sneers, sauntered up the sidewalk. They paused at the store he had entered, and then meandered into the street, kicking stones over the wheel ruts. A stray stone clattered onto the sidewalk outside their hiding place, and one of the boys ran for it. Rosemary drew further back into shadow, but the youth caught the movement like a blue-eyed cat.

"What do we have here?" His voice was a sour tenor. His calloused knuckles whispered as he rubbed his hands together.

Warily, Rosemary stepped into the light. Peter followed her, staying close.

The other boys, their faces grimy, gathered around, gaping at Rosemary. "Well, well!" exclaimed the sharp-eyed leader. "A young maid in need."

Peter nudged Rosemary behind him. "Leave us alone."

The boy huffed. "That wouldn't be Christian of me, would it, now? A young woman on the streets of this mean city, with just the clothes on her back ...." He grinned at Rosemary's halter top. "And not even on your back. Desperate for food and shelter.... Rob Cameron at your service, ma'am. I can help you make a living in this town, for just a small reward."

He reached to touch her shoulder, but she grabbed his wrist instead. "Leave us alone." Her nails dug in. Rob Cameron grunted.

The slowest of Rob's three boys hadn't taken his eyes off of Rosemary's bare back. He guffawed. "You sure are a looker. Would you roll in the muck with just anybody?" He ran his hand through Rosemary's grimy hair, and the air left him as Peter punched him in the stomach.

The boys pounced. Peter's fists flailed, but punches hit home and knocked him on his back. Rob circled the melee, shouting directions and encouragement.

When his back was to Rosemary, she ran at him, putting her shoulder into him and sending him face first into a wall. He crumpled, cried out, and clutched his nose. Blood seeped through his fingers.

Peter shoved his attackers aside and ran to Rosemary. They faced the gang defiantly.

"That ain't no way for a lady to act!" Rob shouted, his voice pinched.

"I'm no lady," Rosemary snarled.

They heard a shout from down the street, and hard soles pounding.

"Police!" The gang scattered, running north.

Rob glared at them. "This ain't over!" He glanced back at the officers, then ran after his boys.

Peter bundled Rosemary back into the doorway's shadow as the constables charged past. Then it was quiet again.

"Are you all right?" Rosemary touched Peter's cheek. "You're bleeding."

Peter flinched, then pulled her hand away. A punch

had broken the skin on his cheekbone. Blood trickled down his dirty face. "It's nothing. I'll heal."

Rosemary smiled. "My knight in shining armour."

Peter laughed. "The damsel in distress isn't so helpless herself."

Then, movement caught their eye and they looked back across the street. The well-dressed man stood outside the store he'd entered, tapping his cane as he stared up the street where the boys had fled. He shook his head. Then he turned on his heel and walked south, cane clicking with each step.

Peter and Rosemary waited until the block was clear before stepping back onto the sidewalk.

"What now?" asked Peter.

"We stick to the original plan." She crossed the dirt street to the open store, then stopped to read the awning. "Toronto-Yorkville Pawnbrokers ... Pawnbrokers! Peter, I have an idea!"

He came up beside her. "What do we have to pawn?" He stared in horror as Rosemary started to pull a ring off her finger. "Not our promise ring!"

"This is no time to be sentimental." She struggled with the gold band.

"But —"

"No buts! It's either this or I sell my hair!" She let out a cry of triumph as the ring came free. Squaring her shoulders, she marched to the pawnbroker's door, pulled it open, and stepped into the dark of the shop.

CHAPTER THREE

~~ :•: ~~

FAITH, HOPE, AND CHARITY

A bell jangled as Rosemary entered. She blinked in the wavering lamplight.

The store smelled of old furniture wax with a hint of stew. The customer area was small, blocked by an oak counter. The rest of the store was given to stacked furniture. Sheets of newsprint pinned to the walls listed watches, jewellery, and other items for sale, with prices written with charcoal. At the back of the room, a man sat hunched by his desk, his face in his hands.

Rosemary cleared her throat. "Excuse me."

The man flinched. "For the love of ...." He was clean-shaven and bewildered. There were lines below his eyes. He raised his soft voice and its hint of Scottish brogue. "We are closed this Lord's Day! Do you not know ...." He saw her and stood up, knocking his chair back. "Good God, woman, you're hardly dressed!"

Rosemary crossed an arm around her chest. "I know.

Can you look at this ring?" She thrust it out to him. He crossed the floor and stared at it.

Peter burst into the shop. "Rosemary, there has to be another way —"

She rounded on him. "Like what? Sign up at a poorhouse? Peter, have you read *A Christmas Carol*?"

"This is not London, England. This is Toronto, Ontario!" He swiped at the ring.

"A fat lot of good that does us when we have no money!"

The shopkeeper cleared his throat. "Excuse me!" Peter and Rosemary stopped in mid-struggle. "First of all, this shop is closed. If the police thought I was doing business, I'd face a fine. Second, how do I know this ring belongs to you?"

"I don't believe this." Rosemary held up her hand, showing the crease the ring had left behind. "I've had my ring on this finger for a year! If I could steal, wouldn't I have stolen clothes?" She spread her arms wide. The shopkeeper averted his eyes.

She grabbed his hand and pressed the ring into his palm. "So, you, look at this ring and tell me what it's worth, and you," she rounded on Peter, "keep quiet until you come up with a better idea of how to find food, clothes, and shelter!"

The shopkeeper looked from seething Rosemary to cowed Peter and back. "Right," he said at last, and he pulled a magnifying glass from the drawer.

"Gold," he muttered. "No diamonds. A claddagh. Oddly stylized. The detail work is ...." He stopped, stared, then dropped his magnifying glass and put a jeweller's loupe to his eye. His eyebrows shot up. "Exceptional! The goldsmith that made this must have had a rock-steady hand! How could you afford such a ring?" He stared at them, then looked back. "Ah, an inscription. 'March 21/08' — odd misprint, that. 'To Rosemary Forever, Love Peter.'"

He looked up. The jeweller's glass fell into his hand. "Peter. Rosemary. Those *are* your names."

Peter and Rosemary nodded.

"This really *is* your wedding ring!"

Rosemary's mouth dropped open. Peter spluttered. But before either could say anything, the shopkeeper thrust the ring back. "I canna take this!"

"What?" gasped Rosemary. "You have to! It's all we have!"

"But to give up your wedding ring?" the shopkeeper cut in. "I know times are bad, but this is a treasure beyond money. I'll not take it from you. As for food and shelter ...," he pulled open a drawer and took out paper, a pen, and an ink bottle, "... there is a church up the street; the priest will help you. With my letter of reference, you may find shelter, perhaps work. What's your name?"

"Rosemary Watson," replied Rosemary. "But —"

The man dropped his pen. "Watson?" he repeated. "Mr. and Mrs. Watson?"

Peter started to say something, but Rosemary pressed her heel to his toe.

The shopkeeper levered up the oak counter and pressed the promise ring into Rosemary's palm. "My name is Edmund Watson. Come back with me."

As Edmund led them through a door to the back, Peter leaned close to Rosemary. "Why did you tell him we're married?"

"I didn't," she whispered. "I just didn't correct him."

"Great! Now I'm Peter Watson."

"Fine, you explain the quaint twenty-first-century custom of hyphenated last names!"

They walked through a long, candlelit hallway. They passed a bedroom doing double duty as a storeroom and went through a door at the end of the hall.

The smell of woodsmoke and stew struck them as they entered a bright, cluttered kitchen. The setting sun caused the shelves and canisters to glow. They heard a bubbling on the pot-bellied stove, and the sound of a woman muttering in the pantry.

Edmund cleared his throat. "Faith, let me introduce Peter and Rosemary Watson." He turned to them. "My sister, Faith."

Peter blinked. "Faith? It couldn't —"

The woman stepped out of the pantry, dusting flour from her hands. She froze. Then her flour-covered arms crossed her chest. She may have changed into a faded brown dress and a frayed apron, but she was still the same woman who'd tended to Peter after the accident. Rosemary swallowed hard.

"We've met," said Peter.

"Yes," said Faith. "I recognize the back of you."

"Um ...," said Rosemary, "sorry about that."

"Faith?" Edmund looked from one woman to the other. "Why do you frown?"

"This was the young couple I found on the street after church," said Faith, not taking her eyes off Rosemary. "The same ones who ran as soon as the constabulary arrived, leaving me to look a fool."

"In our defence," said Peter, "we were facing a hostile crowd."

"Making me look a fool before an audience," said Faith.

"I ... I'm sorry!" Rosemary backed away. "I didn't mean to embarrass you. We'll be leaving —"

Edmund blocked her path. "Faith, these two are destitute; they tried to sell their wedding ring. They are Watsons: family! We must help them."

Faith's expression kept its edge. "We should help the destitute, but I'll not have fugitives under my roof. I demand an explanation." She turned on Rosemary. "Why do you fear the constabulary?"

"Well," said Rosemary. "You saw how people re-acted to us. How do you think the police would have treated us?"

"I would have spoken for you," said Faith.

"And if they didn't listen?"

Faith's glare softened. "All right, I can understand why you may have run, but let me be sure: who are you and where are you from?"

Rosemary bit back her answer. "Uh ... from away."

Edmund stepped around and stood by Faith's side. "You're just off the boat?" He turned back to Faith. "We *have* to help them. Alone in this vast country —"

Faith silenced him with a raised hand. "You do not sound Scottish, English, or Irish." She hesitated, frowning. "You do not even sound American. You're not from here, but where are you from?"

Peter opened his mouth, but couldn't get an answer out. "Away," he said at last.

Faith stepped forward. "Show me your hands." Peter and Rosemary obeyed. Faith examined Peter's fingers first. "You've not done a day's work in your life!" She snatched up Rosemary's hand. "And you have a fine wedding ring. How came you to be in such a state?"

"Did you elope from some dukedom?" asked Edmund. "Are you running from your families?"

"No," Rosemary said. "I won't lie to you. But I won't tell you where we came from, either. You wouldn't believe it. All I can tell you is that we're not criminals, we're just lost. We need help. If you don't want to give it, I'll understand."

Faith looked Rosemary in the eye. Rosemary met her gaze. Silence stretched. Then Faith nodded. "We will help you."

Peter let out his breath.

Faith added water to the stew. "Supper will be ready shortly, but first we must get the stink of the street off you." She snapped her fingers at Edmund. "Get another bucket of water immediately. We have to run a bath!"

"Bath!" said Peter. "That's great! Where ...." He stopped short as Faith dragged a metal tub out of a corner. She stared at the two teenagers standing with their mouths agape.

"Well, go on!" She motioned to the tub. "Decide between you who uses it first. Edmund will be back with water and then you will have the kitchen to yourselves. Leave your clothes by the door, and Edmund and I will have fresh clothes ready when you're done."

"Um," said Peter.

"I ... er ...," said Rosemary.

"I'll return with a towel and soap. Do not dally." And Faith went upstairs, her hard-soled shoes clicking up the steps.

Peter and Rosemary stood in the centre of the kitchen. They looked at the tub. They looked at each other. Peter gulped.

~~ :•: ~~

Rosemary pulled at her collar as she clopped down the steps wearing a brown gingham dress. She felt like she was clad in curtains, strapped in a metal cage. The corset held her so upright, she felt as though her posture was on permanent trial. The skirts hid her feet and the edges of the steps. She kept one hand firm against the wall.

At the base of the steps, she saw Faith hanging clothes near the stove. The woman fingered Rosemary's halter top, stretched out the elastic fabric, and marvelled as it snapped back into shape. Tentatively, she measured the garment against her chest.

Rosemary jumped into the kitchen. "Hi!"

Faith crumpled the halter top into the hamper. "Ah, you are dressed! Let us see how my old gingham fits you."

She planted Rosemary in the centre of the kitchen and spun her around as though she were a clothes mannequin. "You are just my size. I was worried, but now you have a selection of clothes to choose from. And you fill them out very well."

"Thank you." With no mirror, Rosemary could only imagine how she looked. Something between a schoolmistress and a farm wife, perhaps. Probably closer to the former. "How do you think Peter's doing?"

They heard footfalls in the hallway leading to the storefront and Edmund's bedroom. The door opened a crack. "Don't laugh."

Rosemary rolled her eyes. "I won't. Come on out."

The door opened the rest of the way and Peter entered the kitchen. His expression soured and Rosemary knew he'd spotted the quirk in her mouth. She bit her lip, but her shoulders betrayed her.

While Rosemary was Faith's height and girth, Peter towered almost a foot over Edmund. Cuffs bit into his wrists and his trousers ended halfway up his shins. Peter's glare hardened as Rosemary struggled to hold back her giggles.

Then Faith burst out laughing. Peter threw up his hands.

"I'm sorry," said Faith, bringing her laughter under control. "But 'tis the best we can do."

"What am I going to do?" moaned Peter.

"I'll go down to my church tomorrow," said Faith. "I'll see what they have in the poor box."

Peter sighed. "This will have to do, then. One more thing for the shopping list."

Edmund strode into the kitchen, stopped, and looked Rosemary up and down. "Ah! I knew Faith would find a use for those old clothes. You wear them well. Is supper ready, Faith? I could eat a horse!"

At the mention of dinner, Peter and Rosemary's stomachs grumbled. They stood at Edmund's shoulder as Faith inspected the stew, testing it with a ladle before nodding and pouring the ladleful into a bowl. She clopped to the kitchen table without a word, leaving Edmund to ladle out his own bowl and join her. Peter and Rosemary followed. Edmund had his spoon halfway to his lips when Faith cleared her throat and fixed him with a sharp glare. He put down his spoon and leaned forward into grace.

The moment "Amen" left his lips, Edmund attacked his stew, Faith not far behind. Peter and Rosemary were left staring a moment before they took up their spoons. Everybody ate with little thought to decorum. Edmund fetched himself a second bowl.

"Now that we have you clothed and fed," said Faith, cutting off a hunk of bread, "we must talk about shelter."

"But you've done so much for us already," Rosemary began.

"Least I could do for fellow Watsons," said Edmund. He swallowed. "We have an apartment over our store, beside Faith's room. Faith and I used to rent it out, but it's been empty for a month."

"How are we going to pay you back for all this?" said Rosemary.

"I have a suggestion." Faith picked up a sheet of paper from the counter. She passed it to Rosemary.

Edmund peered over her shoulder and said, "Your university application?"

Rosemary blinked. Then she understood. "You're applying to university?"

Faith shook her head. "I'm already attending, I'm only applying for more classes. I take a class here, a class there, fitting things around my work. 'Tis a slow way to get an education. But now you are here."

Edmund stared. "Faith?"

"You can cook?" Faith asked Rosemary.

Rosemary drew into herself. "Some things."

"And you can man a shop counter as well as I could," said Faith.

"Faith," Edmund cut in. "It takes skill to sell in a shop! You know that!"

"I've manned counters before, though," said Rosemary. "I helped staff a library ... where I was before."

"See?" Faith beamed at Edmund. "If Rosemary could take three hours a day, or four, I could take two extra classes and graduate a whole year sooner!"

Edmund sat back. He picked up his spoon and started on his third helping of stew. "Time is one thing. What of money?"

"There is my sewing," said Faith. "I could take on another batch to pay the extra cost."

Edmund grunted. "That solves money. Now we are back to time. More sewing and more study?"

Faith waved Edmund's comments aside. "It means a few late evenings of work, 'tis all."

"You will ruin your eyesight."

"'Tis a small sacrifice."

"'Tis not!"

"What are you studying?" Rosemary cut in.

Faith drew herself up. "I am at the Women's Medical College."

Rosemary set down her spoon. "You're going to be the first woman doctor in Canada!"

Faith's smile widened. "Hardly the first, my dear! I do not have the strength to change the world, but I do have the wit to follow the path cleared by Miss Stowe and Miss Trout."

Edmund leaned toward Peter and gave him a conspiratorial grin. "You see my sister's stubborn streak? Such passion about becoming a doctor! Stay off the subject, my lad, or she'll go on about the vote, next."

"And why should I not have the vote?" Faith thundered. "I voted in the civic election this year. Did the Dominion fall to its knees?"

"That's different," Edmund cut in. "That was just a civic election. You didn't have to trouble yourself about affairs of state."

"Affairs of state?" Faith's nostrils flared. "Affairs of this state can be left to a souse because he is a man? It would do this nation good if landless women *could* vote. Then, perhaps, we could pass temperance and our prime minister might sober up enough to give affairs of state the attention they deserve!"

Edmund was about to continue, but Rosemary cleared her throat. "Aren't your dinners getting cold?"

The siblings stared at their stews. Edmund chuckled, got up, and began clearing away the dishes.

"I apologize for my brother," said Faith. "He likes to antagonize me, though not usually before guests." She shot Edmund a glare, but he kept his back to her.

Rosemary grinned. "When I fought with my brother, it was with pillows."

~~ :•: ~~

Lighting the way with a kerosene lamp, Faith led Peter and Rosemary up the stairs from the kitchen. "I'm afraid you will find the apartment small," she said, "but it has its own tub and stove, and a bed."

"Thank you so much," said Rosemary. She carried her own kerosene lamp and rubbed her eyes with her free hand. "It'll be wonderful to sleep in a bed. I could sleep on the floor."

Two doors fronted onto the landing. They glowed brown in the guttering light. Faith produced a key and unlocked the door closest to the back, above the kitchen. She handed the key to Rosemary. "Here you are. The other room is mine. We're separated by closets, so you won't hear me talk in my sleep."

"I don't think that will be a problem." Peter drooped by the banister rail.

"I'll retire myself," said Faith. "I have to arrive early to register for my new classes. Good night!" She turned down the short hall, closing her bedroom door behind her.

Rosemary led the way into the apartment. There, she stopped dead. Peter bumped in behind her.

Faith wasn't kidding: the apartment was small — one room — and it was bare. A metal tub sat in a corner by a window. A small table held a washbasin, and a single throw rug covered a small square of floor.

The centrepiece of the room was the bed: singular, narrow, laden with quilts, and jutting from the wall into the middle of the room.

"Huh," said Rosemary at last. She closed the door behind them and began undoing the buttons on her dress. "I'm turning in."

Peter stared at her, then strode to the window. "Gee, that's a lot of stars!"

Rosemary threw the corset into the corner with a thump. She breathed deep and rubbed her sides. She blew out the kerosene lamp, leaving the room bathed in the little moonlight that was coming through the window, and slipped beneath the covers. Wearing a camisole and bloomers, she felt more dressed than on a day at school. "Night, Peter."

"Good night."

Rosemary took a deep breath. Then she became aware of the silence in the room, and looked up.

She could hardly see in the dark, but she could sense Peter standing, facing her. Then, taking a deep breath, he turned and stepped to the other side of the room. She heard him stripping down to underpants and undershirt, folding his clothes, and draping them over a straight-backed chair. Then he came over, socks scuffing the floorboards. "Could I have a pillow and a quilt?"

"Sure." She passed them over.

"Thanks." He flopped the quilt onto the floor, fluffed up the pillow, and lay down. "Night, Rosemary."

"Good night."

She stared at the mottled, shadowy ceiling. Her mind whirled too much for sleep. It was one thing to sleep in a strange bed in a strange room, but in a strange time? That took the cake.

But her joints ached. She closed her eyes and breathed deep. Beside her, on the floor, she heard Peter roll over and smack his lips. She faded away. Suddenly, he leapt up with a squeaking scream.

Rosemary sat bolt upright. "What? What? What?"

"There was a mouse!" Peter yelled.

"Quiet," said Rosemary. "You'll wake Faith."

"I don't care! It ran across my feet!"

"What, you've never seen a mouse before?"

"I don't let them in my bedroom, if I can help it." Peter got his breathing under control. "Where are the mousetraps?"

"I don't think they've been invented yet."

"Great!" He threw up his hands. "Just great. Not only am I stuck in the past, but I've got to share a bed with a mouse."

"Well ...." She reached out in the dark and touched his arm harder than she'd intended, but held on. "You could share a bed with me." She froze. That didn't come out the way she'd expected it.

She could hear him blinking. Then he said, "What did you just say?"

Rosemary thought a moment, then took a deep breath. "I'm serious. I know it's a small bed, but it's better than sleeping on the floor. Besides, we're supposed to be married. What's Faith going to think if she finds a second bed on the floor?"

He shook his head. "N-no. I ... I couldn't."

"Why not?"

"It wouldn't be right."

"Would you rather sleep with me or the mouse?"

"You, actually," said Peter. "That's my problem."

Rosemary blushed red to her ears. But she reached out, found his hand, and clasped it. "Peter, I trust you."

He stood a moment, staring, then reached for the covers. Rosemary made room for him, but even with their arms touching, each felt the edge of the bed on their other side. They pressed as close to each other as they dared.

"That was a really girly scream, by the way," said Rosemary.

"Well, it was a mouse," said Peter. "Or possibly a rat."

"Or maybe a raccoon," said Rosemary. Peter elbowed her. She laughed. He laughed too. Then their arms and sides brushed, and they stopped laughing. They stared at the ceiling.

Rosemary took a deep breath. "So ... you remember what we talked about?"

"Yes."

"'We're not ready.' That still stands, right?"

"What do you think?"

"I asked you first!"

They laughed at that. Then Peter said seriously, "I think it still stands."

"Good," said Rosemary.

"Good," said Peter.

Silence stretched. Then Rosemary rolled onto her side toward him. Peter's breath caught. She leaned in and Peter grabbed her shoulder. "What are you doing?"

Rosemary sighed and kissed his cheek. "I love you."

"I love you too," he croaked.

She rolled away. "Good night."

"Good night."

CHAPTER FOUR

~~ ⠒⠂⠒ ~~

FINDING FEET

Peter squatted on the embankment. The wooden construction fence stretched across the creek, black against the moonlight. The ground sloped away, leaving a hole beneath the wall big enough to walk through while stooped.

Rosemary stood beside him. "That's not good for security."

"I watched the place yesterday," said Peter. "You remember the watchman who chased us out two days ago? He's actually the foreman."

Rosemary frowned. "Why would they have the foreman watch the site?"

"I think he lives here," said Peter. "He's got a cabin near the gate. With our luck, he's a light sleeper."

She leaned over and wrinkled her nose. "The creek looks polluted."

"Probably. You ready?"

"Wait a minute. Hold the candles." She passed over a bundle that clattered softly in the silence. Then she pulled up her skirts. Peter almost fell down the embankment. "Rosemary, what —"

She pulled off her overdress and undid the fastenings of her corset. "These things are worse than high heels." She cast the corset aside and stood dressed in chemise and bloomers. She saw Peter staring at her, mouth agape, and glared. "What? I'm wearing lots."

He closed his mouth, then chuckled. "The guy who finds your clothes is going to have a heart attack."

She smirked. "Consider it a parting gift." Then she looked down at the discarded dress and bit her lip. "I wish we could get that back to Faith somehow."

"Here, Faith: thanks for lending me your dress. We don't need it where we're going."

She swiped back the candles. "Let's go."

They half-crawled, half-slipped down the embankment into the creek bed. Rosemary grimaced as the mud sucked at her boots. Peter hushed her and she stuck her tongue out at him. They ducked under the fence and into the construction yard, following the stream toward the open culvert.

The ferns along the creek bed disappeared and the exposed bank was cut back at a neat angle. Gravel rose, followed by a line of bricks on either side of the straightening stream. Soon they were walking between two low walls.

Rosemary looked up at the night sky, then clasped Peter's shoulder and pushed him against the brick wall. He looked at her sharply, then followed her gaze. The words froze in his throat and he drew himself down.

A tall figure stood at the top of the embankment, silhouetted in moonlight.

It was the foreman; had to be. He raised a lantern and shone it across the ditch.

They held their breaths.

The foreman swung the light over their heads, then back again. Finally, he turned away and stalked off, deeper into the encampment. Rosemary touched Peter's arm and motioned at the culvert. They carefully sloshed their way over.

At the opening, Peter took two steps before realizing that Rosemary wasn't following. He looked back and saw her standing in the middle of the stream, staring up at the entrance, her bloomers and chemise glowing in the moonlight, her cheeks almost as pale. Her hands balled into fists.

He came back to her. "You okay?"

She took a deep breath. "Let's go." She pushed into the darkness.

He heard her footsteps steady in front of her, splashing in stray puddles. The water was too shallow to flow, but the bricks were slick and slimy, the stench oppressive. Peter breathed through his mouth. As darkness deepened, Rosemary's steps faltered and he bumped into her.

"You're sure you're okay?" he whispered.

"It's just dark," she muttered. "And wet. And stinky. And dark."

"We'll light the candles as soon as we're a little way from the entrance," he said.

"Are we there yet?"

"Just a little while longer."

Rosemary clasped Peter's hand hard and they pushed forward.

"Why didn't you tell me you were claustrophobic?" asked Peter.

"I've never liked close places, you know that."

"Yeah, but —"

"I told you," she snapped. "It's wet. Stinky. This is not some closet. Or cave. Though I hate caves, too." She halted. "Candles."

"Are you sure?" He looked back. The entrance was a postage stamp of moonlight.

"Now."

He stared at the hunch of her shadow. "Okay. Hold one out."

He patted his pockets for the matches. Rosemary's breathing quickened. Finally, he found them and struck one on the box. And struck again. And again. The air screeched on his fourth try. Light dawned. Peter touched the flame to the outstretched wick. They blinked at the sudden brightness.

Then the match singed Peter's fingers and he

shook it out. The light dimmed to a small flame on the candle's tip.

Rosemary touched a second candle to the first. The light flared up, then faded. They stood in a circle, glowing as though lit by a dying flashlight.

"Got any more candles on you?" asked Peter.

"No."

Peter sucked his teeth. "These will have to do, then. Let's go on."

The brick pipe encircled them, red and black, gleaming with moisture. Rosemary shuddered. Holding their candles close to their chests, they pushed on.

Gradually, a new sound sidled into hearing: a rush of flowing water. They glanced at each other and nodded. A few more steps, and the ceiling pulled away. A breeze brushed their cheeks, and the sound of a rushing stream filled their ears.

Peter took another step, but Rosemary froze. "I can't see."

He turned. "What?"

"These candles," she said. "The light doesn't go far enough."

Peter looked around and saw she was right. Other than a thin circle of light on the bricks around their feet, and a glimmer off the walls of the half-pipe, all they could make out was shadows and a thin, phosphor glow. The cavern echoed with emptiness, black as a blindfold.

Peter swallowed. "Okay. I thought the candles would give us more light than this."

"The wicks are too short," said Rosemary. She scratched at the nib. "If I could remove some of this wax —"

"Careful!"

The candle snuffed out. Rosemary cursed beneath her breath. She touched the snuffed candle to the first, too fast, and killed that light, too. Darkness descended.

They stood for a moment in silence.

"I don't think we've thought this through," said Rosemary, her voice tight.

"No, we're okay," said Peter firmly. "I'll just light another match." He struck one. He struck it again. And again. And again. He grunted, frustrated. "I thought matches from the past would be easier to light. You know, less worries about safety? C'mon you stupid —." The match flared and broke. Peter started, and the broken match and the box slipped from his hand, the box spilling out its matches. There was a splash like rain, and the lit match snuffed out.

"Oops," said Peter.

There was a moment's silence.

"Peter?" said Rosemary.

"Yeah?"

"Oops?"

"I —." He cleared his throat. "I dropped the matches."

"Saw that."

"Yeah."

More silence.

"Got any more?" asked Rosemary.

"No."

Rosemary's breathing began to echo off the walls.

"I think we should go back," said Peter.

Rosemary sloshed upstream, keeping close to the wall. Peter struggled to keep up. "Rosemary," he hissed. "Quietly. You'll wake the foreman."

She spoke through clenched teeth. "Get. Out. Now."

He caught up with her as the moonlit exit pulled into view. He grabbed her and held her as she struggled, a scream building in her throat. "It's okay," he whispered in her ear. "We're there. We're as good as out. Calm down. Be quiet."

She held him. He could feel her heart thumping. She took a deep breath. "It's the dark. I was okay when I had light. We need better light."

"We'll get some. Let's get out of here."

They walked out of the sewer in silence. They kept low. When they passed beneath the hoarding, Rosemary charged out of the stream and lay on the embankment beside her discarded corset and overdress.

"I'm sorry," she gasped. She beat the ground with her fist. "This is stupid!"

He touched her shoulder. "It's okay. We'll do it right, next time. We'll get lanterns ... something that won't burn out. We've got plenty of time. Time's moving slow on the other side of the portal, remember?"

"How can you know?" she said bitterly.

"Theo, remember?" But he couldn't keep his voice from catching. "We didn't hear him shouting after us after we fell through, remember? I'm sure, when we get back, the portal will take us to the exact moment we left. Theo won't know we've gone."

Rosemary closed her eyes. She thumped the ground again.

~~ :•: ~~

It was a tense walk back after Rosemary pulled on her corset and overdress. Peter stared warily at Rosemary's hunched shoulders.

They heard the sounds of waking households as they entered the alleyway paralleling Yonge Street: a shout, a child's cry. At the other end of the laneway, they heard the slap of water on the bottom of a metal bucket.

The shop was dark. They took a moment to clean the mud from their boots and frown at their wet pant legs and bloomers. At least Rosemary's stains were covered by her overdress. They snuck into the kitchen. Together, they crept to the stairs.

The back door banged open. Faith came in, grunting, hauling a bucket over the threshold. She looked up. "Rosemary! You are up early!"

Rosemary closed her eyes wearily. She nodded to Peter, who was hidden by the wall, and turned back to the kitchen. "We're both up. Peter's still getting dressed."

"Help me lift this onto the stove." Faith grasped the rim of the bucket. Rosemary came over and pulled at the metal handle. Together, they hefted it up. Rosemary wrinkled her nose at the brackish, earthy-smelling water. "Ew!" she said before she could stop herself.

"I know," said Faith, opening a hatch in the pot-bellied stove. "The condition of the wells is a disgrace." She poked at the embers with fresh kindling. The fire flared to life. "That is why I always boil the water, no matter what the Public Health Department says."

"Good idea," Rosemary muttered. The water smelled like her damp bloomers.

"Put some in a pot when it boils. There's a packet of oatmeal in the pantry." Faith nodded at a small room in the corner. "I have to fetch my books." She stepped upstairs. Rosemary fought down a surge of jealousy and set about exploring the pantry.

She was stirring a bubbling pot of oatmeal when Faith returned, followed by Peter, who was wearing fresh clothes.

"I am sorry I was such a poor host yesterday," said Faith. "I hardly saw you between your late morning and my late studies. But I must say that this place was kept clean, and I thank you for it."

Rosemary rolled her eyes and said nothing. She hated cleaning, but it was just the excuse she needed to search for and find those candles. Not that anything had come of her sacrifice.

"I see my education is in good hands." Faith gave her a winsome smile. Rosemary bit her tongue.

Edmund entered from the front. "Ah! Breakfast! Good, I'm famished." He pushed forward, grabbed a bowl, and stood waiting. Rosemary realized she had the ladle in her hand. Edmund made no move to take it. She dipped the ladle in the pot and poured the oatmeal into the bowl. He walked away, licking his spoon.

Faith set a bundle of books, tied by a leather strap, on the table. She picked up a bowl and stood waiting. Rosemary served her, too. Then Peter shrugged, picked up the bowl, and joined the line. He frowned at Rosemary's glare. "Um ... please?"

Rosemary slapped a ladleful of oatmeal into his bowl. Peter walked away, wiping a fleck from his eye. Rosemary served herself and joined the others at the table.

Unlike dinner, breakfast was eaten in silence. Peter kept shooting worried glances at Rosemary, which soured her mood even more. Then Faith pushed aside her bowl and stood up. "I have to go to classes. I sign up for my new ones today."

"Off you go, then," said Edmund. "When you are through here, Rosemary," he handed her his dirty bowl, "come up front. I'll show you how to handle the shop."

"Thank you again for the cleaning, Rosemary," said Faith as she swept out the back door.

The room emptied out, leaving only Peter and Rosemary. Rosemary held Edmund's dirty bowl in her hand.

She looked down at it, then swung it at the kitchen table with a shout.

Peter snatched the bowl from her hand. "Woah, woah! Easy!"

"I didn't go off to college so I could keep house," she snapped.

"You're not just keeping house," said Peter. "You're helping Edmund out with his store, too."

She grabbed the bowl back and raised it high, taking aim at his head.

"I'm really, really sorry I said that," he said. "But it's just a couple of days. Until we can get the stuff we need to go back. Okay?"

She lowered the bowl. After a moment, she set it on the kitchen table. "Lanterns, you mean."

"Yeah. And rope, since we did fall in. And maybe climbing gear, if we can afford it."

"We can't afford it."

"Well, maybe ..."

She looked up at him. "You thought of something. Give."

"I was just thinking," said Peter. "We've got food and shelter, thanks to you. I spent all of yesterday staring at the construction site from the top of a hill. Maybe I can be more constructive, so to speak. They hire for odd jobs at the beginning of the day."

Rosemary's eyes widened. "You don't even know how to use a hammer!"

"How hard can it be?"

Her hand went to her cheek. "Oh my God, you're going to die."

"It's a good plan!" he huffed. "It gets us money, and I can scout the site properly. Perhaps even find things, like a lantern, to help us go back."

She sighed. "Just be careful, all right?"

"Okay, Miss Worrywart."

She reached for the bowl again.

"Backing up slowly," he said. Then he turned to the back door. He hesitated there a moment, then turned back. "This may sound weird, but ... doesn't this seem like an appropriate time to kiss?"

Rosemary snorted and shook her head, smiling at last. She came to him and kissed him on the lips. "Have a good day at work, dear." She punched his shoulder softly. "Bring home that bacon!" She gripped the back of his neck. "Don't get hurt."

~~ :•: ~~

"Let me show you how this place operates." Edmund led Rosemary into the front section of the store. He pulled a black, leather-bound book from the desk. "This is the inventory. When we buy goods, we write down when we bought them and how much we paid. When we sell goods, we write down when they were sold and for how much. Understand?"

Rosemary nodded vigorously.

"Now this ...." Edmund set the black book aside and picked up a sheet of rough paper. "This is where you will write down the day's sales. At the end of the day, I take this and add the numbers to the business ledger. Don't worry about the book; it will be my duty to fill it out." He frowned at her. "You *do* know how to work with figures, don't you?"

Rosemary barely kept herself from rolling her eyes. She smiled and nodded.

"Good!" said Edmund. He handed her a pen and a receipt. "Try it."

Rosemary bent over the page. She put the pen to paper and dragged it. Nothing came out. She stared at it. "You're out of ink."

"There's the ink bottle." Edmund pointed to a corner of the desk.

"Ink bottle." She took a deep breath. "Here goes...."

She dipped the pen and brought it to the page. A line of black drips followed her. She tried to wipe the splotches away, smearing the desk and the sleeve of her dress.

Edmund sucked his breath.

Rosemary got a manageable amount of ink and bent back over the page. She pressed the nib on the line and squawked as a pool of black swept over the numbers.

"Here!" Edmund snatched back the pen. "Perhaps *I* should enter the day's purchases."

"All right." Rosemary bit her lip. "But if you do, you should know that you made a few mistakes."

Edmund froze. "Mistakes?"

She pointed at four different spots on the page. "You forgot to carry the four, and twelve nines is one hundred and eight, not ninety-six, and here and here you forgot the decimal point."

Edmund stared at her.

She smiled at him sweetly. "They're perfectly easy mistakes to make."

Edmund turned back to the page and recounted, mumbling the numbers and tapping his fingers. He did the numbers again. Then he stood up. He handed over the pen.

"Thanks," she said. "Do you have a pencil?"

~~ :•: ~~

Step one, Peter decided, was getting past the foreman, who was standing watch at the gate.

Peter stepped up and cleared his throat. The foreman's amber eyes fixed on him and narrowed, but he didn't order him out. "What do you want?"

Peter swallowed hard. "Excuse me, sir, but would you have any jobs available?"

"What makes you think we would?" said the foreman. "Have we signs asking for hired hands? Did you see us asking for workers from the street gangs?"

Peter suspected that the answer was "no." "I could be useful," he ploughed on. "I can keep your books. I know my way around an office. I can read blueprints!" That was a lie, but he figured he could learn quickly.

The foreman turned away. "I'm sure you have plenty to offer, but so do dozens of people not employed here. Look elsewhere."

"But —"

"I'm sorry, son." The foreman didn't meet his eyes. "These are hard times, but there's nothing I can do."

He was about to say something more, when two things happened. A horse-drawn cart laden with timbers drew up to the gate, and the old man caught sight of two slouching boys trying to sneak past. He collared them. "You're late!"

"There was an accident getting here," said one.

"My pa needed me at home," said the other. "He's sick. Very sick."

"My ma's sick, too," the first boy cut in. "On her deathbed, she is!"

"Don't try that on me," the foreman growled. "I've seen how you work. You're never around when there are bricks to be unloaded and your shovels prop up your chins. You were late three times last week!"

Peter looked from this argument to the cart of timbers. He lined up behind the workers grabbing beams and hauled a heavy piece of wood over his shoulder. Turning carefully, he walked past the foreman without staggering.

"Excuse me," he said as he passed.

"Sorry," the foreman began, then stopped short. He stared as Peter shouldered the beam to the growing pile of timbers inside the construction site, dropped his load into place, and helped the worker behind him to unload his beam as well.

"You see that?" The foreman turned on the two sullen boys. "That's the sort of work we like to see here, not your lallygagging! He's worth what the pair of you cost. He works here now. You don't!"

"You can't fire us!" the first boy shouted.

"Yeah! My ma's at death's door!" the second added, before catching himself. "I mean, my pa —"

"Enough!" the foreman yelled. "Go away and do whatever it is you do, except don't expect to be paid for it!"

The two boys started to protest, but thought better of it. Shooting evil glances at Peter, they stomped away.

Peter unloaded his second timber and went back to the foreman. "Thanks. What else do you need?"

The foreman smiled at him. "Can you lay bricks?"

"I can learn."

"Good! My name's Tom Proctor. I'll pair you up with Smith. Mr. ..."

"McAllister," said Peter after a moment's hesitation. "Peter McAllister."

"Well then, Peter McAllister, let's get your name on our rolls and see what else you can do."

He stepped back into the construction site. Peter turned to follow, but stopped when he saw the two boys in the distance. They were talking to a third, taller, sneering boy, his nose in a bandage. Peter recognized him: Rob Cameron.

Peter ducked inside before Rob looked up.

~ ~ ⁝•⁝ ~ ~

Rosemary added water to the stew and chopped in a peeled carrot. With a sigh, she'd settled into stirring when the back door banged open. Faith entered, hauling Peter over the threshold. The young man grimaced in pain.

"Peter!" She rushed over and helped Faith lower him into a chair.

"I found him staggering home," said Faith, flexing his arm and peering at his red and raw knuckles. "I think he has strained himself."

"I told you you'd hurt yourself!" Rosemary slapped Peter across the back of the head.

"Ow!" He glared at her. "I'm all right. It wasn't so bad. I know how to lay bricks now."

"Raise your arm above your head. I dare you."

He scowled. "Don't want to."

"You have overworked yourself," said Faith, setting his arm on the table. "A hearty supper and a good night's sleep and you will be better by morning."

"See?" said Peter. He pushed himself up. "I can do this. Even if they only pay me ninety cents a day, I can do this." He fished into his pocket and drew out five coins.

"That is no slave wage," said Faith. She stowed her books, tied by a leather strap, on a shelf.

"You forgot inflation," Rosemary whispered into his ear. "I was at the butcher's this afternoon. That could buy a good cut of meat." She picked up the coins and slipped them into a pocket in her skirts.

The door opened and Edmund entered, tapping his fingers together and muttering numbers beneath his breath. He brightened when he saw Faith and Peter. "Ah! You're back. Now we can eat! How was your first day at work?" He clapped Peter on the shoulder. Peter gripped the table and whimpered. Rosemary lowered him back into his chair and massaged his shoulders.

Edmund peered into the bowl of stew, stirring it with the ladle. "Is supper ready?"

Faith slapped his hand away. "Rosemary is in charge of this meal. She will tell us when it's ready. Is it ready, Rosemary?"

Rosemary waved at the bowls. "The carrots will be hard, but if you don't want to wait, help yourself."

They didn't wait long. After they'd eaten dinner, Faith stayed to help clean up. Peter reached for the dishes to help, and stopped when he saw Edmund and Faith staring at him. He gave Rosemary an apologetic grin, handed her the dish, and darted upstairs.

As Faith set some dried plates on the shelf beside her pile of schoolbooks, she brushed a piece of paper. Seeing it, she frowned. Then she picked it up and held it behind her back. "Edmund?" He was reaching for the door to the front. He turned around. She gazed at the floor and bit her lip. Rosemary looked up from washing the dishes.

Edmund stared at Faith. His eyes narrowed. "Faith?"

"I applied for my additional courses today."

He sighed. "Show me the bill."

Faith hesitated, then held out the paper. Edmund took it, took a deep breath, and peered at it. His face went red. "Ten dollars? Is this professor teaching you personally?"

Faith's eyes turned to the floor.

"Does the university think I'm made of money?" Edmund threw the paper on the table. "How can it cost so much to teach something people already know? How do they expect us to afford this?"

Peter appeared at the stairwell door.

"My sewing —," Faith began.

"Have you started on your sewing yet?" Edmund shouted. "Have you got your money yet? Maybe you should see your clients and ask for an advance?"

Rosemary flicked suds from her hand. "I'll help."

But Edmund was in full rant. "I pay fifty dollars a year for your education. I already put food on the table and keep a roof over our heads. How can they expect me to do more?"

Faith bit her lip again.

"I said I'll help!" Rosemary shouted.

A stunned silence fell. Everybody stared at her.

Rosemary stepped forward, fished in her pocket, and brought out two quarters. "We never talked about rent. We've been here two nights. How does a quarter a day sound?" She frowned at Peter's look. He turned away and slipped quietly upstairs.

"Rosemary," Faith began. "You already help around the house. We cannot ask for more."

"Faith is right," said Edmund. "We can afford this. We'll afford it, somehow. We cannot take —"

"Take it," Rosemary snapped. "Or, if you don't, then don't argue about money in front of me."

Edmund and Faith lowered their gazes to the floor. Edmund reached out, hesitated, then plucked the quarters from Rosemary's palm.

~~ :•: ~~

Grunting, Peter hauled a folded screen up the narrow stairs. He juggled it at the door of the apartment so he could twist the knob and kick his way in.

Rosemary, who had been slumped on the bed, leapt up as he entered. "Peter! What did Faith tell you about overstraining yourself?" She grabbed the screen and helped him set it down.

"I know." He smiled at her. "But you seemed really down and I thought this would cheer you up. Found it in the basement, actually." He unfolded the screen on stiff hinges and stepped back. "Ta-dah!"

Rosemary pushed her glasses further up on her nose. Before her stood a three-panel screen, with thick canvas stretched over a wooden frame. Asian designs were painted on the canvas. It stood around five feet tall. She looked at Peter.

"A change screen. Thought we could use it," said Peter. "Especially since Faith finally found some night-clothes for us." He pulled a bundle from under his arm and tossed it to her.

She caught it and unfurled a one-piece nightgown of white cotton. She grinned. "We don't have to sleep in our underclothes anymore!"

Peter patted the screen. "And with this baby, I don't have to stand facing a corner while you change clothes."

With a whoop, Rosemary darted behind the screen and, before Peter could look away, began undoing buttons and slipping off her overdress. The screen blocked her from the shoulders down, but Peter took two steps back. The top of the screen became draped with dress and undergarments. Then Rosemary slipped on the nightdress and stepped out into view. "Ta-dah!"

She was clad in a one-piece slip of sturdy, white cloth, laced at the neck and with short sleeves. The slip ran down to just below her knees, exposing her shins and ankles. She wriggled her toes and Peter caught himself looking.

He pulled his gaze away and grinned at her. "You'll make them come back into fashion!"

She tossed him the remaining bundle. "Your turn."

As he got behind the screen, she sat down on the bed to watch. "Other than almost breaking yourself, how was work?"

"Not bad," said Peter, draping his trousers over the top of the screen. "It actually feels good to work with my hands. Well, not physically. But it feels good to build something. It helps that Mr. Proctor's sort of taken me under his wing."

"Mr. Proctor?"

"The foreman. I was right, by the way; he lives in this shed on-site. He has one kerosene lantern. I couldn't find any spares."

Rosemary sucked her teeth. "Those things are expensive."

Peter didn't say anything. He folded his shirt and draped it over the screen.

"I know," said Rosemary. "But Faith and Edmund sound like they need the money. They've given a lot to us, and I feel guilty just taking from them."

"I know." He shrugged on the clothes Rosemary had tossed him, and looked around for the rest of the bundle. He couldn't find anything. He looked down at himself, then stared.

"Peter? What's wrong?"

He stepped from the cover of the screen, wearing a white nightgown in the same cut as Rosemary's. "We didn't accidentally switch, did we?"

Rosemary smirked and patted the sheets. "Come to bed, Miss Nightingale."

Peter rolled his eyes and crossed the floor. As he pulled back the sheets, Rosemary stopped him. "Hey."

Peter looked up. She knelt on the bed and looked him in the eye. "You've been good, these past couple of days. When I ...," she faltered and looked at her fingertips, "... panicked, you were level-headed. You kept me steady."

"It was nothing."

"No." She took his hand. "It's everything. It's terrible being here, but ... it would be a whole lot worse if you weren't here with me."

He looked away. His mouth quirked. "Thanks."

"Thank *you*," she said. And she kissed him.

He kissed her back.

They kissed again.

They paused a moment, and then reached out and pulled each other in. They kissed longer, lingering. His kisses strayed from her lips and over her throat. Clasping him, she leaned back. He pressed her to the bed.

Then they stopped. Peter pulled back. They stared at each other. After a moment, Peter coughed. "So many reasons we shouldn't —"

Rosemary couldn't quite catch her breath. "Level-headed. That's my Peter."

"We should go to bed ... I ... I mean, to sleep."

"Yeah. Sleep. Right."

They stared at each other a moment longer. Then he rolled off her.

As he sat up and put his feet to the floor, she caught his arm. "Stay? Please?"

He looked at her. Smiled nervously. Then he blew out the candle and slipped under the covers.

CHAPTER FIVE

~~ :•: ~~

ALDOUS BIRGE

Rosemary ran downhill, wild and free, the skirts of her blue dress billowing behind her, dancing like marsh light, shimmering with a phosphor glow. The damp grass mushed beneath her bare feet and she laughed to the sky.

Then she looked down and saw bricks lining her path, turning the grass to gravel. The stones bit her feet. She cried out and tried to jump over the bricks, but the line grew into a wall and she bounced off it, back onto the straight and narrow. She ran faster than ever. She couldn't stop.

Water bubbled around her, rising from the gravel and turning her blue skirts black. The bricks rose around her and closed in over her head.

The water cried out, "Release me!"

She ran face first into a metal grate. Her skirts tangled around the bars. The water pressed into her back. She pushed away, desperate, and felt another grate fencing her in from behind. The walls narrowed until she was in a brick-and-metal coffin, black water rising over her chin. She screamed.

The water cried out again, "Release me!"

Her glow flickered and went out.

She woke, gasping. It took a moment to realize where she was, whose arm draped over her, and who snored in her ear. She sighed, levered Peter's arm up, and kissed the back of his hand before slipping out of bed.

Peter rolled onto his stomach. "Turn the water off," he mumbled.

Rosemary wrapped a shawl over her nightclothes. Then she heard a soft knock at the door. She padded over.

Faith was on the other side, holding out a bundle. "Good morning! I meant to give these to you yesterday."

Rosemary blinked sleep from her eyes. "Faith? You already gave us clothes."

She pressed the bundle forward. "These are a little old, but they were my Sunday best, once. I thought you could use these today."

"Why? What's today?"

"Sunday," said Faith, as if that said it all.

"What happens Sunday?"

Faith stared at Rosemary as though she had sprouted horns. Rosemary clued in a second later. "That would be church!"

Faith kept staring.

"Which we go to!"

Silence stretched.

"Every Sunday," Rosemary added.

More silence.

Rosemary snatched up the bundle. "Thanks!"

Faith turned away, casting looks behind her as she went downstairs. Rosemary closed the door and banged her head on the frame. "Stupid! Stupid! Stupid!"

She snatched a dress out of the bundle and tossed the rest at Peter. He woke with a grunt. "Wha—?"

"Get up!" She darted behind the change screen and pulled off her nightdress. "We've got to go to church!"

"But I wanted to sleep in," he mumbled. "What is this, Easter?"

"Just do it!" she snapped. "We're Christians, after all!" She emerged from behind the screen, hoisting a brown brocade dress over her camisole. "Help me with my buttons!"

Peter rolled out of bed, grumbling about rest for the wicked.

~~ :•: ~~

The toll of church bells rolled across the city. Faith walked as though she were pulled to church on a string. Among the crowds, the others struggled to keep up. Rosemary pulled at the collar of her dress. It had been starched to within an inch of its life. Peter slouched, blinking sleep from his eyes. As for Edmund ...

Without breaking step, Faith turned back and glared. "Edmund, come on! You shall make us late!"

Edmund started. His hands were stuffed in his pockets, and he'd been staring at the gaps in the sidewalk. Rosemary nudged him. "You okay?"

He pinched the bridge of his nose. "I had a late night last night."

"Are you *sure* you couldn't use my help with the ledgers?"

He reddened. "No. I'm fine."

The crowds converged on their church — the same church Peter and Rosemary had passed when they first arrived. Rosemary glanced at the crowds in their Sunday best, wondering if anyone would recognize her with her clothes on.

Her eyes tracked to an alleyway between two stores. A group of three boys, barely older than ten, huddled in the doorway, their skin mottled with grime. They frowned at the people in their fine clothes. One of the boys caught her staring and stuck out his tongue.

They hurried up the church steps. Peter held the door for Faith and Rosemary. Faith entered, but Rosemary took the door and nodded Peter inside. Faith looked back. "Edmund, come *on*!" He woke from his reverie.

"Edmund!" another voice called. He froze.

Rosemary stood at the door. A man strode up to Edmund, cane clicking on the wooden sidewalk. He wore a beard and a fine, cream-coloured suit. Rosemary thought he looked familiar.

Edmund stood at the bottom of the steps, hands at his sides, eyes wide, as the man came up and clapped him warmly on the shoulder.

Rosemary frowned and craned her neck to see more, but the crowd shouldered her inside.

As she made her way to the pew where Faith and Peter were sitting and slid in beside them, she cast an eye on the church. It was Presbyterian, just like her own church in the twenty-first century, with no stained-glass windows and no ornamentation save for a cross on the altar, but there was an air of strictness that had no place where she was from. Faith sat ramrod straight in her pew. People packed into row upon row of uncomfortable wood. And something told her that the service was going to be a lot longer than what she was used to — on those occasions when she went to church. Her dress began to itch.

The congregation stood. Peter and Rosemary followed a half-second later. At no cue Rosemary could hear, the congregation burst into song.

"Praise God, from Whom all blessings flow;
Praise Him, all creatures here below;
Praise Him above, ye heavenly host;
Praise Father, Son, and Holy Ghost."

As Rosemary fumbled through her hymnal, she heard Faith mutter beneath her breath, "That Edmund! Where is he?"

Edmund rushed to the pew and slid in, flinching under a dozen disapproving stares. The man he'd talked to sauntered past and took his place two pews down.

Rosemary found her place in the book. Taking a deep breath, she hoped she could get through the service without offending anyone.

~~ :•: ~~

"Faith? Are you still mad at me?"

It was after dinner. Faith and Rosemary were in the kitchen. Faith's books were spread out over the table, but the two women were washing dishes.

"Mad at you? Why would I be mad at you?" Faith's towel blurred as she scrubbed a pot. "Save for the fact that you made me laugh in church!"

"I said I was sorry!" said Rosemary. "It's an old joke. When the pastor goes on about throwing alcohol in the river, you say, 'please turn to the next hymn: Shall We Gather at the River.' How was I to know that would actually *be* the next hymn?"

Faith snorted. Then she caught herself and glared. "So, you laugh in church often, do you?"

"No," said Rosemary. She looked up. "But would God strike me down if I did?"

Faith stared at Rosemary a long moment. Then she sidestepped away.

Rosemary's eyes narrowed. She took a step forward, putting Faith back within striking distance.

Faith took another sidestep away. Her mouth quirked. They giggled, then laughed, as Rosemary stalked Faith into a corner, and then tagged her. "Zap!"

Faith shrieked. "'Zap'? I'll 'zap' you!" She flicked her hand into the bucket of dishwater and sprayed Rosemary in the face. Rosemary gasped and tagged Faith again.

Then someone cleared his throat.

Faith and Rosemary looked up. Peter stood at the back door, staring. Both women were flecked with soap and water, hair straying from their ties.

"Um ... how are the dishes coming?" he asked.

"Come and see!" Rosemary's smile showed her teeth. Her hand swirled the water. Faith beckoned.

"Um ... no." He darted up the stairs.

Rosemary and Faith collapsed into fits of laughter.

"I envy you, Rosemary," said Faith, once her laughter subsided. "You are a free spirit."

"Me?" said Rosemary. "*You're* the one going to medical school."

"And I fret about it all the time." Faith thumped the books lying open on the table. "I worry over classes. I worry over what the men say. You don't care what anybody says. You speak your mind. You can laugh at Pastor Reeve's overlong sermons —." She glanced sharply at Rosemary. "Tell no one I said that!"

Rosemary grinned. "Your secret is safe with me." She frowned. "Have you been having trouble with what some men have said? Does Edmund give you trouble?"

"Edmund? No!" She looked shocked. "He teases me, and goes on about the bills, but he pays them. However, I have had more than one man tell me that women have no place in medical school. This includes teachers and fellow students. Sometimes I wonder if they're right."

"Have your marks been good?"

"Respectable."

"Then you have a place there." She pressed a textbook into Faith's hand. "And while I'm here, I'll help you. I'm really proud of what you're doing."

Faith blushed. "Well, why shouldn't women be doctors?" she said lightly. "We've nursed enough men back to health over the ages." She sighed. "Still, 'tis hard." She put the towel aside and moved to the table, sitting herself down among the books.

Rosemary frowned. "Don't work too hard. You need your rest as well as your study."

"I need to study," said Faith. "And afterwards, I need to sew. To help Edmund pay for this."

Edmund came in through the back door, muttering numbers to himself. He barely looked up as he passed. Faith bent over her books, muttering medical terms. Rosemary watched. Her frown deepened.

~~ :•: ~~

The next day, Rosemary worked the front of the shop when the door jangled. She looked up from the colony of ink blotches on her hands. She found herself staring at the man in the cream-coloured suit who had called out to Edmund outside the church. He had a long handlebar moustache twirled at each end like something you'd expect to see on a circus ringmaster. His eyes were dark pools. He leaned on his ebony cane.

"Good day to you, madam," he said. His voice was cultured, his British accent measured. "What happened to young Miss Watson?"

Rosemary blinked. Then the light dawned. "Oh, you mean Faith! She's in class. I'm filling in for her."

"I see," said the man.

Silence stretched. Each stared at the other, wondering who had dropped their cue. Finally, the man said, "And you are ...?"

Rosemary straightened up. "Sorry. I'm Rosemary. Rosemary Watson."

"Aldous Birge." He held out his hand. Rosemary gave him hers, then stumbled into the counter as Aldous pulled her hand up to kiss.

"Watson?" he repeated as Rosemary rubbed her stomach. "Are you related to Faith and Edmund?"

"Distantly," she replied.

"That explains it!" He laughed. "I didn't think Edmund could afford to hire extra help these days."

Rosemary frowned at the heartiness of the laugh. She cleared her throat. "How may I help you, Mr. Birge?"

"I doubt you could," he said, his chuckles fading. "I have business to conduct with Edmund. May I see him?"

"He's not in," she said. "Are you sure I can't help you? I can find what you're looking for —"

"I'm not looking to buy trinkets." Aldous waved a hand. "I have serious business to conduct. Was Edmund not expecting me?"

Rosemary put on the smile she used at the library for people trying to back out of late fees. "If he was, he didn't tell me. He left *me* in charge of the store, and I'm perfectly capable of —"

"Mr. Birge!"

They turned. Edmund stood, half in and half out the front door, staring at Aldous, his eyes wide. His gaze flicked between Birge and Rosemary. Then he stepped into the store. "Mr. Birge," he continued more calmly. "What brings you here?"

Before Aldous could answer, Edmund cut in. "Rosemary, I fear I forgot to buy bread. Faith will be furious if she finds out. Can you run over to the baker's and purchase a loaf?" He held out a coin.

Rosemary stared. Edmund shifted on his feet and didn't look her in the eye. Aldous stood patiently, waiting for her to leave. She took a deep breath. "Fine." She took the coin and lifted up a section of counter. "I'll be right back."

"Pleasure meeting you, Miss Watson," Aldous called after her.

"Chauvinist pigs," she muttered as she turned up the street. Then she gave herself a shake. What had just happened? So, she'd met a customer she didn't like. What of it? Edmund obviously didn't like him either, so perhaps he'd sent her away so he could speak to him without a lady's "sensitive" ears present. Not that he had to worry on her account.

But something about Aldous nagged at her; maybe his dark gaze, his patronizing smile. The feeling of déjà vu didn't help. "Where have I seen you before?" she muttered as she slipped through the crowds. "And why are you so interested in Edmund?"

~~ :•: ~~

At the end of the day, Rosemary heard Edmund in the hallway, stepping into his bedroom/office. She locked the front door, flipped the sign to CLOSED, and drew the blinds shut. She gathered up the receipts and mail and went in the back.

Edmund's door was ajar and he didn't answer her

knock, so she pushed in and found him hunched over his desk, surrounded by papers, his head in his hands.

"Edmund?" She nudged his shoulder.

He jumped. "What are you doing here?"

She glared at him. "Receipts and the mail. Interested?"

He looked away, wincing. "I am sorry, Rosemary. You just startled me."

"Fine." She handed him the papers. "You okay?"

"Just tired."

"Faith's tired, too." She sighed. "You know, you both could use a holiday."

But Edmund snatched an envelope from the mail and his face lit up. "He wrote!"

"Who?"

He didn't answer. He just tore open the envelope and pored over the letter. Rosemary shrugged and turned away. She stopped when she saw an odd-looking device on a table by the door, all gears and grease. She fingered two wires stretching from it.

"What's this?"

Edmund snapped upright. "Do not touch that! You canna possibly understand —"

But Rosemary followed the wires to the floor, where they ran to a jar of brackish liquid. She held back her hands. "Acid! You built a battery?"

Edmund froze halfway out of his seat. "You know what a battery is?"

"Sure," said Rosemary. "The presence of two metals in an acidic solution generates an electric charge. They taught us that in basic chemistry —." She stopped herself too late.

He stared at her. "That was a very advanced schoolhouse."

She smiled, then turned back to the machine. "So, what are you doing with a battery?"

He coughed. "I ... I like to tinker." He cleared his throat. "I invent things."

She raised an eyebrow. "What are you doing in a pawnshop?"

He drew in a breath. "My uncle James was the inventor in the family. Him and his steam engine. My father, Edmund Watson senior, bought the shop before I was born and always intended that I should inherit it."

"Your father's name is Edmund and he named *you* Edmund?"

"He wasn't inventive. Particularly with names. If Faith had had sisters, they would have been Hope and Charity, in that order."

She smiled. "So, tell me what the machine does, and if it has anything to do with the letter you received."

"How did you know the letter was about an invention?"

Rosemary grinned at him.

"I did write to an engineer," said Edmund. "But not about my Morse code machine. About this." He reached behind the machine and brought out a small box of translucent pink crystals.

"Rocks?" said Rosemary.

"Quartz," said Edmund. "I experiment with electricity and I heard stones such as quartz produce a charge when they are struck or compressed."

Rosemary stopped herself from using the word *piezoelectricity*. She smiled and nodded.

"I've been looking at the potential uses of this phenomenon," he went on. "So far, this is what I have come up with." He fumbled through a drawer and pulled out a gun-like device with two wires for a barrel. He pulled back the spring trigger with a click and a bright spark leapt between the wires.

Rosemary clapped her hands. "You've invented the barbecue lighter!"

"What?"

"Never mind. So, what did the man say?"

Edmund picked up the letter. "He says he is visiting from Montreal ...," he bit his lip, "... tomorrow." He swallowed. "His company has a booth at the Industrial Exhibition and he wants to meet me there, around noon."

"That's wonderful!"

"I am not ready!" Edmund crushed the letter in his fist.

"Edmund, what's wrong? This is the opportunity of a lifetime!"

He shook his head. "No, no. I canna go before Mr. Ballard with only this." He gave his lighter a flick. It crackled and sparked. "I would be a laughing stock."

Rosemary clasped his hands. This time, he didn't flinch at her forwardness. "Yes, you can. It's the best kind of invention: it's simple. You've got notes, right?"

He held up a sheaf of ragged, inky papers.

"There. That's your backup," said Rosemary. "This is perfect. Faith needs a holiday, and you need to work on something other than your shop. So, let's all go down to the Exhibition tomorrow. We'll pack a lunch!"

"Who'll mind the shop?"

"Close it."

"I canna do that!"

"What harm is one day going to do?"

Edmund opened his mouth to object, then closed it. After a moment, he gathered up his papers and put the "barbecue lighter" beside them.

Rosemary beamed. "It'll be great. I'll tell Faith." At the door, she hesitated. "One thing: what *is* this Industrial Exhibition, anyway?"

~~ :•: ~~

"Faith, I'm sorry. I didn't know the engine would spark like that."

Rosemary stood beside Faith, a hand on her shoulder, as the woman leaned against a stall, her face pale. Around them, the crowds chattered, the stall owners called, and, in the distance, a pipe organ tooted its music.

"That *thing*," gasped Faith, pointing to where they had come from, "is a fire hazard. It could well be the creation of the devil. People are not meant to be pulled around by something other than horses or steam!"

Rosemary moved closer to Faith to avoid the crowds streaming off the temporary wooden platform. A train stood on the tracks beside it, with seats on open platform cars and an electric motor for an engine. The crowds off, the train backed out of the station buzzing like a hive of bees. Sparks flashed off the wheels and the third rail onto the wooden platform, dangerously close to the legs of the passengers. The engineer, Rosemary noted, wore thick gloves.

"It's okay," she said, patting Faith's shoulder. "We're here now and we're safe. These engines are the way of the future. I'm sure they're safer than they look."

Colour reappeared on Faith's cheeks, but she looked away. "I feel foolish. Do you think Edmund saw my fear?"

Rosemary looked back. Edmund was watching the train go. He was bouncing on both feet. "Marvellous! To see Van Depoele's design tested here! Marvellous!"

She patted Faith's shoulder. "I don't think he noticed." She stepped over to Edmund. "Don't forget your appointment."

Edmund looked up, showed her his envelope of

papers, and patted the device in his pocket. He gave her a nervous smile. "I'm ready."

Rosemary looked around. "Where's Peter? He's got the food."

"I saw him heading toward the game stalls," said Faith.

Rosemary blinked. "Oh dear. Peter and a carnival. Bad mix. I'll go look for him. You go on; I'll meet up with you at your presentation!" She darted into the crowd.

She'd realized what the Toronto Industrial Exhibition was as she rode the streetcar over. She'd gone to its modern descendant — the Canadian National Exhibition — and there wasn't much difference between the two. The Industrial Exhibition had different showcase buildings and an impressive Crystal Palace, but had the same crowds as the twenty-first century Ex — people shouting and laughing and kids speeding around the legs of their parents. Rosemary marched past the stalls, looking for Peter.

"Madam! Madam!" cried a showman. "I can guess the year you were born!"

Rosemary grinned and rolled her eyes. "I don't think so." She marched on.

She heard the sound of a ball smacking against a wooden wall and she found Peter standing in front of a stall, looking disappointed. "Oh, bad luck, young man," said the stall owner. He handed Peter a ball as big as his hand. "Have another go." Peter took the ball and reared back to pitch. A row of milk bottles stood as targets. "Peter!" she called, and he flinched.

"Don't do that! You'll throw me off my game."

"Peter, we didn't come here for you to be fleeced by the carnies."

He scowled. "I can beat this game. I'm almost there." He hefted the ball in his hands. "I'd do better if this ball wasn't so imbalanced. I'd almost think these games are rigged."

"Of course they're rigged!"

"Just two more sets of bottles and I've got my prize." Peter threw. The ball thumped against the back of the stall.

"Oh, bad luck," said the stall holder with a smile. "Have another try. Just another nickel."

"Peter," Rosemary growled.

He drew the ball to his lips, then whispered to her. "Have a look at what I'm playing for." He nodded at the stand. "Second shelf, near the middle."

Rosemary looked. In the middle of a shelf of tacky bric-a-brac was a brass lantern, straight off a ship. "Peter! It would be cheaper just to buy it."

"Oh really?" He clasped the ball. "I've just figured out how these balls tack." And he reared back and threw. The pyramid of bottles came down with a crash. The stall owner's knuckles whitened on the counter.

Rosemary watched Peter snatch the ball from the now-reluctant stall owner's fingers. She pursed her lips, then shrugged. "All right. When you've done fleecing this guy, meet us by the lake for lunch."

She turned away. Behind her, she heard a crash of falling bottles and a cry of joy.

~~ :•: ~~

Rosemary entered Machinery Hall, a building built like a cross with a clock tower rising from the centre. Inside, people flocked around booths showing the latest inventions. Rosemary found Faith after a few minutes of searching. "Hi!" she said as she came up. "Where's Edmund?"

"Meeting his friend." Faith nodded. Rosemary looked across the aisle and saw Edmund shaking hands with a middle-aged man with salt-and-pepper hair and a bushy moustache. As she approached, the man gave Edmund a curt nod and said, gruffly, "I'm afraid I have to leave soon, Mr. Watson, so let us see what you have."

Edmund opened his envelope and passed over the sheaf of papers. He was reaching in his pocket for his barbecue lighter when someone called out, "Edmund!"

Edmund flinched. Aldous Birge sidled through the crowd, cane clicking.

"What a surprise to see you here," said Aldous. "Business must be good if you can close the shop."

Edmund didn't say anything, so Rosemary stepped forward. "Mr. Birge?" she said evenly. "What brings you out here?"

"Business, of course," said Aldous. "After all, I am a businessman. I have no time for pleasure."

Rosemary's smile hardened. "What sort of business, Mr. Birge? Anything specific?"

Aldous looked away demurely. "You needn't trouble yourself about specifics. It would be a bore to a young lady such as yourself."

"Yes," said Rosemary. "I'm sure you wouldn't want to make us uncomfortable."

"Mr. Watson?" The man with the bushy moustache cleared his throat. "If you please, I do have a train to catch."

"Of course, Mr. Ballard." Edmund fumbled through his pockets, then realized Ballard was holding the papers he was about to refer to. He took them back and spread them on the table. Aldous came to peer over Edmund's shoulder. Rosemary stepped forward and casually shouldered him away.

"I —." Edmund's voice trembled and he coughed. "I have been investigating the electrical properties of stones like quartz, and I have tested how they discharge electricity when they are struck."

"The phenomenon is known," said Ballard, peering at the papers.

"I have quantified the behaviour of the stones." Edmund pointed at a chart. "And here I show how the electricity can be channelled. The process is reversible, so a mechanical action can produce an electrical current, and the current can reproduce the same mechanical action elsewhere. Fine-tuned enough, and almost anything can be transmitted electrically and replicated at the other end of a wire. Most interesting, is it not?"

Ballard looked up. Rosemary could see no sign of whether he was fascinated or bored. "An ... interesting body of work, Mr. Watson, and some interesting theories. Do you have any practical application to show for this?"

"Uh ...." Edmund ran his thumb over his fingers. "Yes ... this." He fumbled in his pocket and brought out the lighter. "Striking the crystal here," he said, pointing at the trigger, "sends an electric current through the wires so the other end ... uh ...," he waved his hand over the device, his words gone, "... does this." He pulled the trigger, and a spark leapt between the wires.

Some of the crowd watching this display jumped, and there were a few mutters of surprise and appreciation. Neither Aldous Birge nor Ballard moved. Edmund stood as though he had a mole on his nose and everyone was staring at him.

Ballard rubbed his chin. "Most ... interesting, Mr. Watson." He flicked open a pocket watch. "But I'm afraid I must leave now. Write and tell me more about your invention. You know how to reach me?"

"Uh ...." Edmund stood staring. Aldous slipped away into the crowd. "Yes, Mr. —"

"Good," said Ballard. "I shall contact you ...," he

considered, "presently. Good day!" He tipped his hat, stepped out of the booth, and walked away.

Edmund watched him go. Rosemary watched Edmund. She bit her lip.

~ ~ :•: ~ ~

"That was humiliating!" Edmund moaned. He sat on the grass, his head in his hands.

"It's okay!" Rosemary reached out to pat his shoulder, hesitated, then drew her hand away. "Mr. Ballard seemed interested."

"He was just being polite!"

"There, there, Edmund," said Faith, setting out the basket of sandwiches. They sat on a blanket spread over a patch of grass overlooking the lake. Picnickers surrounded them. Behind them, the Exhibition hummed. "If Rosemary said it was all right, it was all right. Isn't that right, Rosemary?"

Peter strode up the hill, hoisting the lantern and a brass telescope. "Hey, check out the great stuff I won!"

Rosemary straightened up. "It wasn't enough that you won the lantern?"

He grinned. "You should have seen his face. He gave me the telescope on the condition I stop playing. It's great! I can see all the way across the lake. I was watching this cargo ship heading into dock; clear enough I could see the crates." He put the telescope to his eye and looked out to the lake, then frowned. "It vanished. Must have pulled into something. It was going so fast, I thought it was going to crash." He looked past her. "What's wrong with Edmund?"

She sighed. "His presentation didn't go well. He lost his nerve the moment that Birge guy showed up."

But Peter had spotted the blanket spread out with food. "Ooo! Lunch!" He brushed past her.

Rosemary started to say something, but caught sight of Aldous Birge walking through the crowds. She was hit by another wave of déjà vu. "Excuse me," she said, and she strode off the green.

She slipped through the crowds amongst the stalls and the shooting galleries, keeping Aldous's cream-coloured suit in sight. She dodged laughing kids speeding around the legs of fairgoers. Birge left the crowds at the end of the midway and Rosemary held back, watching him as he crossed a small patch of green free of fairgoers. She was about to follow when someone strode out from between two tents. She ducked back behind cover.

Aldous Birge stopped to greet Rob Cameron. The boy's nose showed purple around his bandage. The two talked, and Aldous nodded and patted Rob's shoulder. Then he turned away, heading for the fairground's exit. Rob watched him go, then turned toward the fairgrounds, heading straight for Rosemary's hiding place.

She ducked back, darting between two stalls. She held her breath as she waited for Rob to pass. The crowds bustled back and forth. Then Rob slipped through into the space between the two stalls and almost walked into her. He stared, and she could see the wheels turning. He doesn't recognize me with my clothes on, she thought.

But then it clicked. He glared. "You!"

He advanced on her, his hands balled into fists. Rosemary noted that they were some distance away from the crowds, but she pushed herself away from the wall and faced him.

"Take one more step," she said, her voice level, "and I'll break your nose again. And then I'll scream. What do you think the people out there will think?"

Rob stopped in his tracks. He looked over his shoulder, then turned back. He didn't advance any further. "You're spying on me, ain't ya?" He jabbed a finger at her. "You'd better keep your nose away from where it don't belong, or I'll break it off."

Rosemary stood her ground. They glared at each other a moment longer before Rob turned and stalked away. Rosemary watched him go, then let out her breath when he stepped out of sight.

CHAPTER SIX

~~ :•: ~~

SAY GOODBYE

Rosemary kicked open the door to their apartment and hauled a steaming pail of water over the threshold. Peter dropped his book and scrambled up from the bed. "Rosemary, what are you doing?" He helped her set the bucket on the floor.

"Running a bath," she puffed. She nodded to the tub that sat by the window. "Help me pour this in."

They hauled the bucket to the tub and tipped it over. The metal rattled. The water filled it to a depth of three inches. Peter frowned. "Not much of a bath."

"There's another bucket on the stove downstairs," said Rosemary. "Bring it up." Peter left. A moment later he was back, and there were six inches of steaming water in the tub.

"That's all there is," said Peter.

She shrugged. "It'll do. It won't be a soak, but it'll be nice to have hot water on my skin for once."

"Uh ... yeah." He coughed, then turned for the door. "I'll be back in half an hour."

"Where are you going?"

He turned back. "What do you mean 'Where am I going'? You're having a bath."

"We need to talk." She pushed the bucket aside. "Compare notes. Did you find a second lantern?"

He looked at her, incredulous. "Bath."

"Oh, for heaven's sake!" She dragged the change screen in front of the tub and stood behind it. "What did you think I was going to do?"

Peter stood a moment, mouth open to object. Then he closed it. He picked his book up off of the floor and lay down on the bed to read. "Go on."

Rosemary rolled her eyes. She gathered up her nightclothes and soap and set them on the floor beside the tub. Then she paused, staring at the steaming tub and rubbing her chin. It was too small and too round to stretch out in. She shrugged and started undoing the stays and fasteners of her dress. She draped these over one panel of the change screen.

"I found a backup lantern," said Peter. "In Tom's scrap heap. It's battered, but it'll do. I'll ask Tom for it. Tell him I can fix it up."

As she worked, the moon came out from behind clouds and shone through the window. The change screens glowed white. The tub threw a dark shadow against them. The water gleamed. Smiling, Rosemary tested the water, and then she slipped out of the last of her undergarments. She eased herself into the tub with a sigh. She knelt and ladled water over herself with a metal cup. "That's good. I found a place where I can buy rope and some climbing gear. We can afford it, too. We're as good as home."

"Home," said Peter. He took a deep breath. "You know, I'm going to miss this place."

Rosemary sloshed water. "Miss this place? You *like* laying bricks and hauling lumber?"

"It feels good working with your hands." He sounded affronted. "You feel like you're creating something."

"By burying a river alive?" She bent forward, dipped her hair, and splashed water over her head. Rising, she tossed her hair back, picked up the soap, and began lathering.

"You're right," said Peter. "We should just concentrate." He stopped, then cleared his throat. "Concentrate on getting back home and not think of how much that'll leave Faith and Edmund in the lurch."

Rosemary grimaced. "I know. I wish there was some way we could repay them." She stretched up an arm and lathered under it. She ran her fingers through her hair and bent down to rinse. "I will miss this place," she said, sitting up. "It's like our first apartment. It'll be hard going back and being a two-hour drive apart."

"Yeah." Peter cleared his throat again. "I know what you mean."

"You okay?"

He coughed. "Just a frog in my throat."

"Don't get a cold on me. I'm not trusting the medicines of 1884."

She rinsed off the soap and scooped the warm water over herself. Satisfied, she stood up, stretched, and looked for a towel.

There was a thump beside the bed.

She frowned. "Peter?"

"Dropped my book."

She huffed. "Peter, I forgot to bring the towel. Bring it over?"

Peering over the change screen, she saw Peter surface, towel outstretched, his eyes averted and his cheeks reddened. She smirked. He slipped the towel over the change screen and darted back to bed.

"It won't be so bad," she said as she dried herself off. "Two hours isn't too far. We'll be able to see each other on weekends and there's always the telephone and the Internet." She rubbed the towel over her hair.

"Yeah," said Peter. "But it's not the ...," he stopped short, then continued huskily, "the same."

"We need to be sensible. We've had fun playing house —"

Peter drew in his breath. "We're not just playing house."

"I know." She stepped out of the tub and dried her ankles. "But that doesn't mean we're ready to live together permanently."

Peter stayed silent.

She listened to the silence. "Peter?"

"Yeah," he said at last. "Yeah, you're right."

She tossed the towel away and pulled on her nightdress. Emerging from behind the screen, she grabbed a comb and started working it through her wet hair. "You going to have a bath?"

"No." Peter kept his nose in his book. "I sponged myself down by the washstand."

"Shame to waste the water."

"Too tired. Just want to go to sleep."

She shrugged. "Suit yourself." She turned from the mirror and froze, her comb caught halfway through her hair.

The change screen blocked the tub and the window from sight. The moon shining through the window, however, set the canvas screen aglow. Against this the tub — and anything in it — stood as a clear silhouette.

She looked at Peter.

He rolled onto his side and pretended to be asleep.

She finished combing her hair and slipped into bed beside him. Silence stretched. Then, without warning, she slugged him in the shoulder.

"Ow!" said Peter. "Sorry."

Despite herself, Rosemary chuckled.

~~ :•: ~~

The next day, walking along College Street, Rosemary blinked to see Faith sitting on a patch of grass, finishing the last of her lunch. Faith got up, brushed the crumbs from her skirts, and turned toward a stone building with tall, Gothic windows.

Suddenly she stopped, brought up short by a young man in her path. Faith made to step around, but the man blocked her. Rosemary ran toward them.

As she closed in, she heard the man sneer. "A woman has no place in medical school. She has no place as a doctor!"

"Let me pass." Faith's voice was curt, tight. She tried to sidestep him again.

"A woman's place is in the home, cooking and cleaning for —"

His voice cut off with a cry as Rosemary sailed into him, knocking him into the muddy street.

"Oh! I'm so sorry," said Rosemary. "It's the glasses! I'm so nearsighted and just a foolish little woman! Here, let me help you up!" She offered her hand, and stepped on his chest.

"Rosemary!" gasped Faith.

"Oh! Did I do that?" Rosemary exclaimed. "Let me help you up again."

The man crabbed away in a spray of mud. "Get away from me, you vixen!"

There was an authoritative clearing of the throat. They looked up to see a constable sauntering toward them. "What seems to be the problem here? Is this man bothering you?"

Faith and Rosemary glanced at each other. In unison, they shook their heads.

The constable blinked. "Are you bothering this man?"

Faith flushed. Rosemary scuffed a pebble with the toe of her shoe.

The constable began to chuckle. He turned to the sodden man. "Be off with you, lest these ladies teach you a lesson you'll not soon forget!" His chuckle exploded into laughter.

The man scrambled up, red-faced, and walked away as quickly as dignity would allow.

The constable tipped his hat to Faith and Rosemary. "Ladies." He strolled away.

"Well, that's one advantage to being a defenceless female." Rosemary rolled her eyes. "They don't arrest you when you defend yourself. Are you all right, Faith?"

"Rosemary, how could you?" Faith looked at her in shock.

Rosemary stared back. "Faith, he was harassing you!"

"And you responded with simple violence!"

"I wasn't violent! Much. What, you were just going to let him badger you?"

"I don't know. But I don't need you to fight my battles." Her expression softened. "Thank you. It was ... trying, facing that man."

Rosemary clasped Faith's hand. "You're welcome. So, how are classes?"

Faith's eyes went wide. "Oh my word! I'm late!" She ran for the front doors, pausing only to turn and wave before rushing inside.

Rosemary looked up at the building and sighed wistfully. Then she turned back toward College Street.

Later, walking with her basket laden with groceries and a coil of rope wrapped in paper, Rosemary blinked to see a well-dressed man emerge from Edmund's shop, putting on a top hat. Edmund darted after him, protesting, but the other man stared coldly, shook off Edmund's restraining hand, and strode away through the crowd.

Edmund's shoulders slumped. Then he turned and almost walked into Aldous Birge. They stared at each other. Aldous extended his hand. Edmund sagged again, and clasped it. Aldous grinned, clapped Edmund on the shoulder, and followed him into the shop.

Rosemary stared. Then she walked past the shop, around the corner, and through the alley, entering the house by the back door. Setting her basket aside, she crept into the hallway and strained her ears, but Aldous was already gone.

~~ :•: ~~

Rosemary dropped the receipts on Edmund's desk. "Not bad. Five sales. The most we've had all week."

Edmund said nothing. He slumped over his desk.

Rosemary frowned. "Edmund?"

He looked up. "Thank you, Rosemary." He stashed the receipts in a folder and turned away.

She touched his shoulder. He tensed, and she pulled her hand away. She took a deep breath. "Edmund ... how's business?"

He looked away from her. "Business ... is fine."

"Are you sure about that? I may not see the ledgers, but I can add in my head. Those five sales we had made for a good day. Can we last very long on the bad days we've had?"

Edmund sat silent. Rosemary decided she didn't care how forward it was, and reached for him again. "Edmund —"

"Rosemary, leave me be!" He knocked his chair back. "Do not forget that you and Peter are guests under my roof! I'll not have you prying into my personal affairs."

She caught herself on a desk. She glared. "I know I'm a guest, Edmund, but after these past couple of weeks, I thought we were friends. Friends worry about each other, and I'm worried about you. Faith's worried, too. If you don't want our friendship ..."

Edmund stared at the floor. "Forgive me, Rosemary. I ... You are a good friend. I'm sorry I spoke so harshly."

"I forgive you," she said. "Now answer the question: Is business all right?"

He rubbed his forehead. "Rosemary, please —"

"If you don't want me to worry, show me I don't need to worry!"

He chuckled tersely. "So it's proof you want. Well, here!" He pulled two documents from a drawer and thrust them at her. "Look!"

She peered at the type, the signatures, the stamped seal of the City of Toronto. "A business licence and tax receipt ..."

"Paid in full." Edmund's voice rose in triumph. "Could I have afforded that if I was destitute?"

She peered at him over the top of the documents. "No."

"No." He laughed again, sourly. "There is plenty of profit in the misery of others."

She smiled tightly. "You don't buy peoples' wedding rings."

"No, but there are plenty of things I do buy. Heirlooms, fine furniture, sentimental artifacts bought to keep the creditors at bay. 'Tis a thankless job. I'm a vulture."

"Then why don't you quit?"

"And do what?"

"Work on your inventions." She nodded at the geared Morse reader behind him. The barbecue lighter was nowhere to be seen.

He sat down heavily. "You mock me, Rosemary."

"No, I don't."

He snatched up a pile of papers lying by the machine. "To think I even wrote a patent application! I was a fool.

Faith can aspire to better herself, not me. She can be a brilliant doctor! I shall always be a lowly pawnshop owner." He tossed the papers into the wastebasket.

He flinched at Rosemary's look of horror. "I ... I'm sorry, Rosemary. I am tired, that is all." He faced his desk. "I'll deal with the ledgers tomorrow. Go to bed now, lass."

The set of his shoulder told Rosemary to go. She walked to the door and stood there, looking back.

Then, in one quick movement, she knelt and snatched the patent papers from his wastebasket, slipping them under her arm.

"Good night, Edmund," she said as she closed the door behind her.

Edmund did not reply.

~ ~ : ● : ~ ~

A kiss woke Rosemary from watery dreams. Her eyes fluttered open. She saw Peter leaning over her, a sheepish shadow.

Her eyes narrowed. "Kissing me in my sleep now?"

"I had to wake you up," he said. "It was the gentlest way I could think of."

She kept her narrow-eyed stare on him.

He drew into himself. "And ... I couldn't resist. Sorry. It's midnight. The others are asleep. You ready to go?"

She leaned back with a sigh and studied the ceiling. She felt strangely sad. In two weeks, she'd made two good friends, and had shared a bed with Peter. Faith and Edmund would be long dead by the time they got back to the present. Then she and Peter would head off to different universities in different cities. She wouldn't be able to sleep next to Peter unless they made special arrangements.

Then she thought of her friends and family. Hot running water. And she and Peter *could* make special arrangements ...

She sat up and swung out of bed. "I'm ready."

~~ :•: ~~

They stepped out of the alleyway onto College Street, carrying a lantern each. Peter carried the grappling hook while Rosemary had the rope coiled over her shoulder. The breeze caught at her skirts. They walked, lanterns creaking as they swung, their hard-soled shoes clicking on the wooden sidewalk. As they approached the construction site, they slowed.

Work had progressed up the creek and the hoarding had moved with it. Checking to see that the coast was clear, they darted across the sodden open ground and ducked into the shadow of the temporary wooden fence. They followed it to the north end of the construction site. This had also moved, but the creek still crossed the hoarding through a wide hole. Peter started forward.

"Wait up," said Rosemary. She passed her lantern over to him, then grabbed the back of her skirts and kilted them up between her legs, tucking the hem into her waist. She looked up and caught Peter staring. "What? You try keeping a dress clean in all this muck."

Peter's lips pursed. "Last time you just stripped down to your underwear."

"Well, that was different."

"How?"

"Well ...." She blinked. "It just doesn't feel right this time." She stopped. Then she slapped her forehead. "I'm worried about showing too much leg. I've been in the Victorian era too long. Let's get out of here!" She grabbed back her lantern, pushed past him, and climbed down into the creek.

"When I get back," she muttered as she sloshed through the pools of water, "I'm going to a beach somewhere. And spending all day wearing a skimpy bathing suit. Or maybe a bikini."

"Can I come?"

Without looking back, she swatted at him and hit him in the stomach.

He chuckled. "Imagine the look on Theo's face when he sees us. You're sure we couldn't get our old clothes back?"

"I think Faith burned them."

"Too bad."

As they approached the round mouth of the tunnel, Peter tapped her on the shoulder. "Quiet here," he whispered. "Tom Proctor's cabin is near here and I'm betting he's a light sleeper."

Rosemary felt a shadow fall across them and she started. She thought she saw a silhouette in front of the setting moon, but when she looked up, the sky was clear. She looked back at the tunnel, its mouth open wide. She swallowed.

Peter leaned close. "You okay?"

Rosemary took a deep breath. Her knuckles whitened on the handle of the lantern. "Let's go." She stepped past the veil of moonlight into the dark.

The brick tunnel enclosed them. There was not even the phosphor glow to light their way. The soft flow of the creek became a persistent gurgle and they heard the slosh of their steps echo back at them with a tinny edge. Rosemary breathed through her mouth to avoid the smell. Her heart thumped. The water seeped over their laced shoes and soaked their feet. She reached back for Peter's hand and found it in the dark. He gave her hand a squeeze.

"You sure you're okay?" he whispered. The walls caught his voice and whispered it back to them.

"Just. Keep. Going."

"We can light the lanterns if you want."

"Later." She sucked in a breath. "We have to be further in. So nobody sees us."

She stumbled on the uneven ground and pitched into the wall. The brick pipe curved. Slimy stone brushed her cheek. Rosemary squeaked. She shoved away from the wall and almost fell. Peter caught her and held her close.

"I hate being like this," she mumbled into his shirt.

"Maybe we should light the lanterns now?"

She swallowed. "Yeah. Sure. Let's do it."

Peter handed her his lantern and fumbled around for matches. He struck one. The air screeched and flared up. She blinked in the sudden brightness.

He took the lantern and pulled open a panel. He touched the match to the wick. The light guttered low, then brightened and steadied. The air glowed around them. The brick pipe glistened red and black.

Peter waved out the match and lit another from the lantern. He lit the other lantern while Rosemary held it. The light brightened until Rosemary was nearly dazzled.

He smiled at her. "Better?"

She felt the tightness ease from her shoulders. A little. She looked ahead. The tunnel stretched in either direction, ending in disks of darkness. "How much further?"

"Not far." Peter hefted his lantern. "I hear the big stream."

They started forward. The trickling sound beneath their feet was overlaid by a steady, rising rumble ahead of them. A breeze brushed their cheeks, cool as a cave.

Then the ceiling of the brick pipe ended and they were in a cavern.

They stood in a half-pipe, the rough rock walls vaulting above them. The cave glittered grey. Stalactites dripped from the ceiling. Peter and Rosemary stared, mouths agape.

"This is under the city?" Rosemary breathed.

"I'm surprised no one's selling tickets."

The half-pipe stretched along the cavern floor, ending abruptly at a brick trench. Grey water rushed past.

Peter handed his lantern to Rosemary, then he hauled himself over the pipe wall, staggering on the sandy ground. Turning, he grasped first the lanterns, then the gear, and then Rosemary to join him. They found, untouched, the footsteps they'd left in the sand when they arrived. They followed these tracks back, shining lantern light over the walls and the ceiling, looking for signs of a cave-in. Several minutes passed before Peter stopped and pointed. "There!"

Rosemary looked. Across the gurgling trench, they saw scattered stones running down to the river. The scree led up to a dark hole in the ceiling. It wasn't far for someone to fall. "We've got to cross that river."

"Good thing we've got the grappling hook." He tied it to one end of the rope and began swinging it over his head. He cast it across the trench and dragged it back. It snagged on the brick edge of the trench and held tight. Peter passed the rope to Rosemary. "After you!"

She looked at the stream — slower and shallower

than when they'd first arrived, but still knee deep. "I'm going to get this dress wet."

"You could wash it at Theo's place."

"Like I'm going to keep this dress!"

"Well, aren't you?"

She stared at him. Then she broke into a grin. She turned back to the stream. Holding the rope, she jumped in and used it to pull herself against the current. A few minutes later, both she and Peter had arrived on the other side of the stream. They stumbled to the cavern wall.

It was definitely a cave-in. Rosemary's breathing quickened. "Theo!" she cried.

Peter covered his ears. "He still can't hear you! Different time speeds on either side, remember?"

"Come on!" She scrambled up the scree. The wall sloped up and there were plenty of footholds. Adrenaline pushed Rosemary forward, even as Peter held back, bracing himself to catch her if she should fall.

She poked her head into the hole and stopped short with a cry. Her lantern slipped from her fingers, fell past Peter, and exploded on the river's brick lip. The flames licked the surface before dying out.

"What is it?" Peter scrambled the rest of the way and caught her as she slumped. "Rosemary!"

She clutched her forehead. "I hit my head!" She looked up and snatched at Peter's lantern. "Give me light! Hurry!"

"Careful!"

He shone the light above her. It bounced against the hole in the ceiling. It was just an indentation. Rosemary brushed her hand over the unbroken rock inside the hole. "It's solid." She looked at Peter, her eyes wide and her cheeks pale. "It's not here."

He turned, shining the lantern across the cavern ceiling. "This is the only ...." He stopped himself. His face grew pale as well.

"We're stuck here!" She gasped.

"Rosemary, no, listen to me!" He grabbed her. "You don't know that. We've only just started looking!"

"Where else can we look? Peter, what are we going to do?"

He put his hand to her mouth, but it was the sudden tension in his shoulders that silenced her. He was looking at the stream, listening. He snatched the lantern and blew it out.

"What are you do—." Then she saw it: where the buried river left the cavern, the tunnel glowed with orange light. Voices echoed, coming closer. A boat pulled into view, pushed upstream by a man hoisting a pole like a gondolier. Two other men sat in the boat, the one in front casting lantern light over the cavern walls.

"The boat's scraping bottom," said the gondolier. "If His Nibs wants to take this route, he's going to have to put wheels on the boat."

"Keep quiet and keep mapping," said the man holding the lantern.

"Why should I?" said the third man in the boat, holding a lap desk on his knees. "I know where we are! I've been through this cavern twice. The last time, I could have walked it and not gotten my shoes wet."

"You're going to walk it if you don't shut it," said the man with the lantern. "Unless you want to put up gaslight, I'll want to trust your maps. Where is this new pipe?"

"Two hundred feet forward north, on your right," said the cartographer.

"North?" scoffed the man with the lantern. "What does the compass say?"

"North," said the cartographer.

"Check the compass!"

The gondolier pulled something from his pocket. "North," he said at last.

The lantern man grumbled.

Peter and Rosemary stared as the boat pushed upstream. A few minutes later, they heard a voice cry out, "Found it! On your right!"

"Just where I said it would be!"

"Good. Let's go back."

"Wait," said the cartographer. "His Nibs wanted the tunnel explored."

"His Nibs wanted the tunnel *found*," said the lantern man. "We found it. That's all we're going to do. The pipe is dry. Do you want to drag the boat along it?"

There was more grumbling, then silence. A moment later, the boat floated downstream into the tunnel. The glow from the departing lantern flickered, faded, vanished.

~ ~ ⦙ • ⦙ ~ ~

It was a long, silent trek back. When Peter and Rosemary struggled out of their muddy boots and snuck back in to Faith and Edmund's kitchen, the moon had set. Back in their room, Rosemary slumped into a chair and stared out the window.

Peter draped his dirty trousers by the washtub, then stared at Rosemary's drooping shoulders. He came up beside her and touched her cheek. "Hey."

She looked at him, a shadow behind her gaze. He knelt to face her. "Look, we're not beaten yet. That portal has to be there somewhere. We'll find it. We won't be here long, okay?"

Her smile was hollow. "Okay."

He sighed and turned to bed. Slipping beneath the covers, he fluffed his pillow and stared at the ceiling. After a minute, he looked back at the window. Rosemary hadn't moved.

"Rosemary, it's late. Come to bed."

"I will," she muttered. But she didn't move. She stared out at the city until the sun rose and the buildings came back to life.

Chapter Seven

~~ :•: ~~

TWO MONTHS LATER

Rosemary woke gasping. She blinked at the ceiling, then heard Peter snoring in her ear. She relaxed. She wasn't drowning.

"Stupid dream." She pushed him aside and slipped out of bed.

~~ :•: ~~

After breakfast, Rosemary stood before her mirror, brushing out her hair. The brush crackled as she passed it through the strands.

Her hair was not the only thing that had grown; Peter's commute was one hundred yards longer, as work had progressed up the creek. He'd complained about it at breakfast.

The breeze from the open window rippled the night-clothes she'd draped over the privacy screens. Leaves scattered up the laneway. Rosemary sighed, set the brush aside, and twisted her hair back with the ease of long practice. She frowned at the way loose strands dangled down the back of her neck.

"Too long," she muttered. Then, with a sudden inspiration, she darted out of the apartment and knocked on Faith's door. "Faith, could you help me?"

Faith muttered something. Rosemary took that as an invitation and opened the door. She started to see Faith look up in shock and shove a bundle behind her back.

"I thought you said 'come in'!"

"I'm sorry; 'tis nothing. You only startled me. How may I help you?"

Rosemary turned around and pointed at her unmanageable bun. "Could you help me put my hair up, like the way you do it?"

Faith got up and loosened Rosemary's hair, running her fingers through the long strands. She clucked appreciatively and twisted plaits through her fingers. "Long enough at last. Don't you know how to wear it up?"

"I know it sounds strange, Faith, but my hair has never been as long as it is now."

Faith grunted. "You have strangeness about your very being. I've grown used to it."

Rosemary chuckled, and Faith began coiling her hair and pinning it into place. After several long minutes of work, she turned Rosemary around. "Is all well, Rosemary?"

Rosemary blinked. "What?"

"You seem troubled. Come, now; you have lived under this roof for two months. Did you not think I would notice?"

Rosemary turned away. She stared out Faith's window at the bustling crowds on the street below. At last she said, "Back home, this time of year, my family would get together for a thanksgiving feast. My grandparents would visit, the days would be just starting to cool, and the leaves would be turning. You could smell it in the air. I can smell it now, but my family isn't here."

Faith turned Rosemary around again and hugged her. Rosemary cradled her chin on Faith's shoulder.

"Shall we have a feast this Sunday?" asked Faith.

Rosemary laughed and let go. "You don't have to do that on my account, Faith."

"'Tis no account," said Faith. Then she stopped. "The truth of the matter is, Rosemary, that I've grown used to having you and Peter here. Our talks, your strengthening words — you're like a sister to me."

Rosemary smiled hesitantly. "I've never had an older sister before."

"Well, I have never had a sister."

"But a feast? How can we afford that?"

"I assume we will use the same funds with which Edmund purchased the material for my spoiled surprise."

"Huh?"

"What you caught me at when you came in here."

Faith picked up a bolt of fabric — sturdy, red, and silky. Compared to Faith's used clothes, it shone. "He surprised me with it today. There is enough for two dresses, so I resolved to make you one."

Rosemary stood agape before finally saying, "Thank you!"

"I had hoped to surprise you, but since you have found out, I may as well measure you properly." Faith pulled a fabric tape measure from her sewing box. "Arms wide!"

Rosemary grinned as she stood like a clothier's dummy and Faith took her measurements. But one thing nagged at her. "Edmund *gave* you this fabric?"

"Such extravagance is unlike him," said Faith. "But our clothes were getting a little worn. I shall make the most of it, though. My sewing skills may not be much, but I promise you that you shall have a dress that will last you for years."

Faith was so engrossed with her measuring that she didn't see the colour drain from Rosemary's cheeks.

~~ :•: ~~

In the kitchen, Rosemary knelt over the washboard, scrubbing clothes vigorously. Tears trickled down her cheeks and her breath came out in sobs. She'd stopped to wipe her nose on her sleeve when Peter burst in through the back door. "Funny how you appreciate working half days on Saturday," he said. "What's for lunch?"

Rosemary turned away. "Hello, Peter," she gasped. "There's bread and a little cheese in the pantry."

Peter frowned at her hunched shoulders. She sniffed, and he drew back in disbelief. "Rosemary ... are you ... crying?"

She sniffed. "No!"

"What happened?"

"Faith's making me a dress!"

There was a pause. Peter blinked. "I thought Faith was an excellent seamstress."

Rosemary burst into tears.

Peter backed away in shock. Then he pulled her close and wrapped his arms around her. "I'm sorry," he murmured. "Whatever it was I said, I'm sorry. Don't cry!"

Rosemary dried her eyes. "It's not you, Peter. It's just — I ... I'm being stupid."

He held her out at arm's length. "What happened?"

She cleared her nose. "I went to Faith to help me with my hair and I caught her hiding a bolt of fabric. I asked her about it and she told me it was a gift. She was making me a dress."

Peter nodded. "And you're upset with her because ..."

"I was so happy," said Rosemary. "But then Faith said that the dress would last me for years. Years! The moment before, I was missing my family so much, and the next moment I was so happy to be here, in this house. Happy for new clothes. I'd forgotten my parents in Clarksbury! I don't want to be here for years! We've got to go back now!"

He sucked his lips. "Okay. We can try."

"Try? The last time we tried was a month ago! Let's do it tonight!"

"It's a cold night. It might not be the best time."

"It's only going to get colder!"

"Rosemary, I —"

She pulled away from him. "What are you trying to say?"

He took a deep breath and avoided her eyes. "Rosemary, we've gone back to the sewers three times, and each time we found nothing."

She turned away. Her knuckles tightened on the table.

Peter went on. "I looked all over that cavern. The only sign of a cave-in was that hole we keep banging our heads on! We can keep trying if you'd like — maybe Faith won't notice our clothes getting filthy every other week — but ...," he took another deep breath, "what if we can't go back?"

Rosemary said nothing.

"You know, things could have been worse."

"How?" Rosemary whirled around. "How could things have been worse?"

Peter swallowed. "We have a roof over our heads and three meals a day. We've got jobs. Better this than dying on the streets, or living in a poorhouse."

"Oh, I suppose that makes up for the culture shock. Or non-culture shock!"

He stared at her. "Why are you being like this? I'm just saying things aren't so bad —"

"Aren't so bad?" Rosemary gasped. "You're asking me to live in a world where I can't vote, can't get a decent job, where Faith gets harassed for going to medical school. You're asking me to live in a world of tuberculosis and cholera. You expect me to be happy here?"

"Well, if we don't have a choice, yes!" Peter snapped. "Instead of moping about, you could go to school —"

"How? This household can't support *two* women attending university!"

"Maybe if you wait for Faith to finish, you could —"

"Study what?" She clapped her hands. "Oh, I know! I'll take up physics and discover radium! Eat your heart out, Madame Curie! Everything I dreamt of being is gone! I've no family, no career, nothing to look forward to —"

"We have each other!" Peter bellowed.

Silence fell as Peter and Rosemary stared at each other, both breathing heavily. After a moment, Peter continued quietly. "We have each other. I know you miss your family. I miss them too, and my uncle, and all our friends. But if we can't go back, at least I can say that there's one thing I'd miss most of all, and it's standing here in front of me. You are the only home I need, Rosemary."

She looked away, and bit her lip. Then she looked Peter in the eye. "It's not the only home *I* need."

Her eyes went wide the moment the words left her lips. Peter stared at her. Silence stretched again. Then he turned toward the back door.

"Peter, I —"

He shot up a hand. "Don't!" He stormed out, leaving Rosemary staring. She covered her face with her hands.

~~ :•: ~~

Peter barged through the crowded streets, hands in his pockets, scowling at the boards of the sidewalk. He followed the sun as his mind whirled over Rosemary's words, her anger, and the pain it had left behind.

Yes, they were far from home, with no friends or family to turn to, but at least they were together. They could get through this together.

Only, she didn't think so. He wasn't good enough for her.

The sun passed behind houses. The shadows lengthened. But Peter didn't slow down. It was only when he heard the stride and stop of the lamplighter as he went from lamp to lamp, igniting the small streams of gas, that he noticed that the crowds had gone. In the quiet, Peter began to really think.

You know, it's harder for her to live here than you, he thought. *If I work hard enough, I can be anything I* want — even a journalist, if I put my mind to it. What can she do? She can't vote for another forty years, and it's hard enough studying biochemistry without having to do it when the field hasn't been invented yet, not to mention the fact that Rosemary going to science school would be blazing a path as bold as Faith's. She can basically be somebody's housekeeper or somebody's wife. She didn't sign up for that.

He looked back the way he'd come, and Rosemary's glare filled his mind's eye. Her rebuke filled his ears. He dug his hands in his pockets and stormed off across the dirt street. Sure, she hadn't signed up for this, but neither had he, and yet here they were. If they couldn't go back, they'd have to make do. Why couldn't they make do together?

He walked until his stomach growled. Then he stopped and looked at his surroundings for the first time. The sky was navy blue. He could barely make out the street signs in the shadows of the row houses.

"Herrick and Muter?" he muttered. "Where's that?"

He frowned. You're a Torontonian, Peter. You used to walk these neighbourhoods. You knew these streets.

But that was a hundred years from now. It might as well be another city. He thought about turning back, but decided to hold off. Maybe he'd get something to eat first. Row houses still surrounded him. There was still a lot of city left to go, surely. There must be a place nearby where he could grab a meal. He set off toward the setting sun.

Two blocks later, he reached the end of town. He stared across a farmer's field, shielding his eyes against the sun. The wind blew across the stubble of threshed wheat. His stomach grumbled again. He didn't have a jacket.

"Okay," he said. "I guess I go back."

He turned around. The last of the sunlight disappeared. Lights in the surrounding windows guttered and were blown out. Curtains were drawn. The wind flung the first flecks of rain in his face. He blew on his hands. The street signs told him nothing.

"What did they do, rename everything? Where the heck is Hope Street?"

The houses didn't look at all familiar. Even the lamplighters were gone. He was utterly alone.

The wind gusted. The flecks of rain turned to flecks of snow. He shivered. Then, turning a corner, he found himself in pitch darkness. The lamps had blown out. He peered about, straining to see the sidewalk in front of him. He laughed tersely.

"Way to win an argument, Peter," he muttered. "Storm out and die of hypothermia."

He drew a shaky breath. It wasn't as bad as that. It really wasn't. He was just lost and alone.

He stopped. Lost and alone. So that was how Rosemary felt.

He leaned against a lamppost. He took a deep breath. "I'm sorry, Rosemary."

He looked up and around. The houses were dark shapes and nothing more. He wasn't just lost, he was completely lost. The sky had clouded over; he couldn't even see stars. He decided to look for lamplight, but couldn't see any of that, either. All the lamps on the street had blown out.

"I could really use some help right now," he muttered.

Then a glimpse of light caught his eye. He peered into the distance, down the street. The silhouettes of houses and street lanterns were more distinct there, backed by a faint phosphor glow, like marsh light. Frowning, he stepped forward, tripping on the uneven sidewalk, but making for the faint light.

He walked for two blocks before the first lit gas lamps came into sight. Then, as he approached, they went out. Peter stopped and stared. The faint, marshy glow was still before him, indistinct as a cloud. His frown deepened. Then he shrugged, and pushed forward again. As he approached the next lamp, it too extinguished.

Peter felt a coldness in his chest. "What's going on here?"

The phosphor glow waited for him, beckoning. He struck off after it, letting it lead him. It was at least taking him deeper into the city. He walked ten blocks. The wind did not let up. Peter's shoulders began to shake.

Then the glow came to a stop. Peter approached. It clung to the last gas lamp like St. Elmo's fire.

"Okay." Peter clenched his teeth to keep them from chattering. "Where have you taken me?"

"Peter?"

All at once, the gas lamps flared back to life. He looked away, blinded. When he looked back, the street was lit by its normal flickering glow. He stood beside a patch of grass, beside the hoarding around the construction site. Tom Proctor stood at the gate, waving his lantern. "Peter? Is that you?"

Peter stumbled across the packed earth to the construction yard's gate.

"Peter! What are you doing out so late?" demanded Tom. "My God, you're half frozen. Come in, this instant. I have a fire."

At the mention of fire Peter perked up, and darted toward Tom's cabin like a moth toward flame.

~~ :•: ~~

Rosemary rolled over in her sleep. Her arm flopped out and dangled off the edge of the bed. It took her a moment to realize what was wrong with that. She felt around the covers. "Peter?"

No response.

She fumbled for her glasses and sat up. She peered into the dim, moonlit room. "Peter?" She was alone.

She slumped back into bed and closed her eyes, but she couldn't stop her mind whirling back over their argument. She pictured Peter standing before her, grinning inanely. "You know, Rosemary, when life hands you a lemon, you make lemonade."

"What if life hands you sand?"

"You make glass."

"What about broken glass?"

The picture shattered. She saw Peter glaring at her, hurt. "I know you hate it here, but what choice do we have?"

She didn't know, but her points stood. They might belong together, but they didn't belong here.

She lay back and stared at the dark ceiling. No sleep here. She rolled onto her side and stared at the wall. Her mind whirled over the moon shadows on the patterned wallpaper. She rolled onto her stomach and tried to breathe through her pillow. It smelled of him.

She sat up again, hugging her knees to her chest. After a moment, she threw off the covers and slipped out of bed.

In the darkness, she stumbled into the water bucket. It clattered, but didn't splash. The bottom was no more than damp.

"Oh yeah," she muttered. Peter usually filled it. "Silly me."

She pulled a shawl from the clothes screen and wrapped it around herself. Slipping out of the bedroom, she tiptoed past Faith's door, silent on her bare feet.

As she descended the steps to the kitchen, new sounds invaded her thoughts. She slowed, listening.

She wasn't wrong. She heard the hiss of something flat and heavy being dragged. It stopped with a thud and a choked-off curse.

Rosemary overbalanced and grabbed the railing. She righted herself, but couldn't stop from putting her foot solidly on the next step. It creaked. The voice below hushed.

Silence stretched as two sets of ears listened to each other. Then, in the kitchen below, footsteps turned and hustled away. A door clicked shut.

Rosemary crept down the remaining steps and stumbled into the now-empty kitchen. Peering around in the moonlight, she turned and walked right into a wooden box. She doubled over on top of it. Then she pushed away, glaring at the box and rubbing her belly.

The box was a crate made of planks. Words were stencilled on each side, impossible to read in the moonlight. She tried to lift the lid, but the top was nailed down.

The door to the basement sailed open. Rosemary leapt back. She gasped in relief when she recognized the shadow. "Edmund! You startled me!"

"What are you doing here?" he growled.

"Couldn't sleep," she replied. "Thought I'd come down for a glass of water. You?"

He hesitated and swallowed, then came forward into the moonlight. "Couldn't sleep either. I thought I would work."

They leaned on the box across from each other. Rosemary tapped the planks. "This your work?"

He nodded. "Brought it up from the basement."

She gave it a tentative push. It was lighter than it looked, but bulky. "It must have given you a lot of trouble getting it up the stairs."

He shrugged. "The exercise will help me sleep."

"I suppose." She looked at him. "What's in it?"

"Merchandise."

"What kind?

"Watches," said Edmund. "From a bankrupt warehouser. I thought I'd sell some."

"Need help with it?"

"I'll manage."

She yawned. Grabbing a mug, she dipped it into the water bucket and took a long drink. Looking up, she saw that Edmund hadn't moved.

"You're just going to stand there?" she asked.

He blinked at her. "No."

She stared at him. She set the mug aside. "Good night."

She gave the crate one last glance as she headed up for bed.

~~ :•: ~~

Peter wilted into the heat of the wood stove. Tom Proctor sat down across from him and unscrewed a metal flask. He took a swig, and then offered it to Peter.

Peter stared at it. "No thanks."

"Go on. It's not what you think."

He took the flask, sniffed it, then took a sip. He stared. "Apple cider?"

Tom chuckled. "You thought I was imbibing whiskey? I wouldn't last long at this job if I couldn't keep a clear head."

Peter took another sip, then handed back the flask. "Thanks."

"I have some stew as well," said Tom. "You need something warm in you after being caught outside this night. What were you doing out so late?"

Peter curled into himself. "Walking."

"Where to?"

"Nowhere."

Tom laughed. "Ah! I've walked to nowhere many a time. Sent there by my wife as often as not."

Peter looked up. "You're married?"

"I was, rest her soul." Tom sighed. "Yes, she sent me on plenty of errands to nowhere, but they were still good times. Sometimes I just needed my space."

"Or she needed her time," Peter muttered.

"Bad argument?" asked Tom.

"Yes."

"She'll forgive you."

"You sure?"

"Do you love her?"

"Yes!"

"Does she love you?"

Peter hesitated. He curled into himself again. "I … I don't know. I think so."

Tom patted Peter's shoulder. "If the answer wasn't a definite 'no,' it's probably 'yes.'"

Peter looked up, hopeful. "You know this?"

Tom nodded. "Forget what they say about men being the head of the household, son. What you have in a marriage is two people under God, and you're both ornery. But that's the way God made you, and you have to be patient with that. You have to understand."

"I'm beginning to." He drooped. "You really think she'll forgive me?"

"Ask her yourself." He got up and dished out a plate of stew. The cabin held a cot, a trunk, and a shelf of books. The room was small enough to be lit by a single kerosene lantern.

Peter stared at the surroundings. "Do you really live here?"

"Until the work here is done," said Tom.

"What will you do then?"

"Look for more work, I suppose." Tom sat back on the cot. "I've been with the university for years, helped to build King's College, taking whatever work they had to offer. Even in the worst of times there are buildin that need to be built, and rivers that need to be buried. There may still be work for somebody as old as me."

"What will you do when you retire?" asked Peter.

"Retire?" Tom's laugh was like a gunshot. Then he grew more serious. "I have a little money saved up. Not much, but it will cover me for a year. I have a son in Kingston, with a good wife and a young son of his own. I hate to be a burden, but perhaps when I hang up my cap, I shall live with them. And maybe sooner than later. After this creek is buried, my job here is at an end."

As Peter stared, Tom's eyes glazed over. He stared out into the construction site, and back in time. "You wouldn't know it, but this creek, Taddle Creek, used to be a treasure to the university. I picked berries here. As part of their initiation rites, the students would duck freshmen in the pond we just drained. That joke wasn't nearly so cruel twenty years ago. Less than a month from now, this creek will vanish forever."

"Why bury it in the first place?"

"It was in our way," said Tom. "And then there was the cholera and the typhoid ... though, I remember, the river held no cholera before the city stretched this far."

He stared out onto the grounds again. "I've seen this city change so much. I was born the day the Town of York became the City of Toronto; ten years before, mind, but the very day. There were ten thousand souls in the city that day; now I hear there are almost nine times that number. We could walk across the city and not be footsore, then; no need for streetcars to carry us." He took a swig from his flask. "All these people, pushing to the university, beyond the university. Where will it end?"

Peter accepted the flask and took a swig. "Where indeed. But if you feel this way, why are you helping to bury Taddle Creek?"

Tom shrugged. "A man has to make a living. Besides, I've lived a lot of my life near this stream. It seems fitting that I should be there at the end. At least someone will tell its tale." He tensed. "Quiet!"

Peter blinked. "What —?"

"Somebody is sneaking through the site." Tom clasped a thick stick that stood propped by the door. He motioned for Peter to follow.

The ground was crusted with frost. The cold rain had stopped and the sky was starting to clear. A waning moon cast the site in shadow. Peter and Tom crept between the piles of timber.

"How did they get in?" muttered Peter.

"Not by the gate," said Tom. "I've had my eye on it the whole time."

"How —"

"They're in the river bed." His voice rose to a shout. "You there!"

The lip of the embankment surrounding the creek was before them, the slight rise a shadow in moonlight.

"I know you're in there!" Tom shouted. "Nobody has stolen anything from here on my watch and tonight will be no different. Come out now and I'll send you away with a bug in your ear and no more! Don't make me come in after you!"

There was silence. Tom's voice echoed back at them.

"I'm warning —." But before he could finish, four shadows leapt into the moonlight like soldiers from a trench. They barrelled into Peter and Tom, knocking them over. Peter grabbed an ankle and twisted. His attacker yelled and sprawled. Peter grabbed the flailing legs, and a boot slipped off into his hands. A kick landed solidly on his shoulder. His quarry scrambled up and ran limping after its friends.

Peter got up to follow, but stopped at the sight of Tom bent double. "Are you okay?"

Tom nodded. Peter helped him up. "I got somebody's boot, at least," said Peter.

Tom peered at it. "A common workboot. That tells us little."

"What did they want?" asked Peter.

"Who knows? Tools, lumber, anything they could sell. They did not take anything, however, that's important."

"Maybe." Peter looked at the embankment surrounding the river. "Maybe it was the river they wanted."

"Hmm?" Tom looked at him.

"Just thinking out loud," said Peter quickly. "You're sure you're all right?"

Tom waved him away. "Yes, yes. Don't go on so."

But Peter stayed close as Tom headed back to his cabin. When he was sure everything was all right, he said goodbye and headed home.

~~ :•: ~~

Rosemary rolled over in her fitful sleep. Something made her open her eyes. Peering through the gloom, she recognized the shape at the foot of the bed, hunched and nervous. "Peter?"

"Rosemary, I'm ... I'm sorry." He took a deep breath. "I know being here is harder for you than for me, but ... Look, if we can't go back, I'll do everything I can to make this easier, I promise. Wherever we are, I want us to be happy. Will you forgive me?"

She opened her arms to him. "Come here and let me show you how much you're forgiven."

Peter's grin lit up the dark.

~~ :•: ~~

Rosemary dotted her letters and set the quill pen to rest in its holder. She reached for a cloth, then noticed that her hands were clean of ink splotches, for once. Come to that, so was the paper. "Huh!"

Outside, men and women strode past on Yonge Street, their boots muffled by the falling snow.

She looked up as the door chimed.

A tall gentleman doffed his hat. "Good afternoon, madam. Is Mr. Watson available?"

"He's out on business," said Rosemary. "Can I help?"

"Perhaps." The gentleman unfolded a slip of paper. "My associates took delivery of a consignment of watches — one gross. This is the paperwork."

Rosemary looked at the slip.

"For the most part we are happy with the product," the gentleman continued, "but we did find a handful of timepieces that did not work. Mr. Watson said I could return these for credit." He set a paper bag on the counter.

"I'll have to ask Edmund," said Rosemary.

"I'll leave the watches with you and return, then. You may contact me at this address." He handed her a card for a jewellery store on King Street. He tipped his hat to her and left.

Rosemary watched him go, then looked in the bag. It contained a half-dozen narrow boxes. She took one out. "Let's see what's wrong with you." She sat at the desk and rifled through the drawers until she found the jeweller's loupe, which she'd modified with a loop of wire so it could rest on her head and hang over the right lens of her glasses. She held the pocket watch by its chain and peered at the back, opening the cover with a jeweller's screwdriver.

She stared at the insides for a long moment, then grabbed the back cover and peered at it through the lens.

"Peter!" she shrieked.

She was the only one in the store.

~ ~ : • : ~ ~

An hour later, Rosemary was pacing the kitchen like a caged animal. She stopped as the back door opened.

Peter entered, blowing on his hands and stomping the snow from his feet. He beamed when he saw her, then squawked as Rosemary grabbed him by the wrist and hauled him upstairs.

Rosemary slammed the door to their apartment. "Look at this!" She couldn't keep still as Peter stared at the watch in bewilderment. "One of Edmund's customers returned this as defective merchandise. Look at the writing on the back! I just found out why it doesn't work!"

Peter peered at the back of the watch. He froze. Slowly, he raised his gaze to her. "Made ... in Taiwan?"

Rosemary nodded. "The battery ran down."

CHAPTER EIGHT

~ ~ : • : ~ ~

BORROWED TIME

Peter sat down. He almost missed the foot of the bed. "There's another portal."

"And somebody knows about it," said Rosemary.

"But how?" Peter threw the watch aside. "If more people know about this, how come we've heard nothing?"

"Clearly, they didn't tell anyone." Rosemary began to pace. "They didn't get a scientist. They didn't tell the government. They just went to the future and brought back watches — cheap watches."

"You think it's Edmund?"

Rosemary shook her head. "He would have put two and two together and told us; remember the date on our wedding ring? But it's somebody Edmund knows and deals with." She stopped pacing and snapped her fingers. "Birge. He's been like Edmund's shadow, and Edmund's had 'guilty conscience' written all over him ever since Birge showed up. Maybe Birge is a time criminal."

"A time criminal," said Peter with a hollow laugh. Then he sat up. "Actually, try time *gang*. That night Tom and I ran into those burglars, they didn't take anything. They were just interested in the river. Then there were those people in the boat who floated past us that night we tried to get home. It can't be coincidence that they were rowing up the river that brought us here."

Rosemary tapped her chin. "Maybe 'His Nibs' is Aldous himself. With a name like Birge, he's got to be an evil mastermind."

"An evil mastermind who finds a portal to the future and brings back cheap watches?"

She swatted at him.

"So, what do we do?" he asked.

"You wear the deerstalker hat and I smoke the pipe," said Rosemary.

"Rosemary, be careful. We don't really know what we're dealing with."

"A group of people who know a way for us to get home."

"Who may be a criminal gang. With Aldous Birge at its head and a bunch of people, including Rob Cameron, as his henchmen."

This brought Rosemary up short. "Hmm. Yes, we'll have to be careful. You keep an eye on the construction site, and I'll wait until Edmund steps out of the shop and then search the place for clues." She gave Peter a sidelong look. "We have to try, right?"

Peter nodded. "Oh, we'll try."

Rosemary vibrated with renewed energy. She bounced on the balls of her feet. "I don't believe it, Peter! We actually have a chance!"

He grinned at her, opened his arms.

Rosemary bowled him onto the bed.

~~ :•: ~~

The next day, with Faith taking an exam and Peter at work, opportunity presented itself.

Edmund looked up as Rosemary entered the front part of the shop. "Ah, Rosemary! I have some business that takes me from the store. You can mind the counter, can you not?"

Rosemary's smile widened. She took up a quill pen and stood ready.

Edmund took his hat from the stand. He fidgeted over it as he backed out the front door.

Rosemary stood behind the counter a moment. Then she darted to the door, checking up and down the sidewalk to make sure the coast was clear. Finally, she hung a sign reading "The Shop Will Open Again in Fifteen Minutes" on the door, shut it, and drew the blinds.

She clapped her hands. "Right! Where do I start?"

She chewed her lip, and then snapped her fingers. "Edmund's bedroom!"

Edmund's bedroom/office had always been cluttered, but it now looked as if it had been hit by a whirlwind. Boxes were stacked about haphazardly. Edmund's geared invention was blocked from view, its battery disconnected and shoved in a far corner.

Rosemary shuffled around the boxes, looking for the top of Edmund's desk. She picked up a folder and flipped through an inventory list.

"Cups, plates, watches," she muttered. But no dollar values, and no return address. She set down the folder and reached for the desk drawer, staring when it would not budge.

She knelt and peered at the lock. It was a firm bolt, little hope of picking it; not that she knew how. She couldn't wrench open the drawer without a crowbar, and she didn't want to be *that* obvious.

She stood up, frowning. The ledgers were under lock and key. Edmund had been secretive before, but this ...

She looked at the inventory lists, blinked, and looked closer. Cups, one gross. Plates, two gross. Watches, two gross. There was a long list.

A gross was one hundred and forty-four items. Were they all in Edmund's bedroom? No; Rosemary shook boxes at random: they were all empty. Could they all have been sold? She didn't think it likely. So, where was the merchandise?

Then she remembered Edmund bringing the great box into the kitchen. "Basement!"

She strode into the kitchen, snatched a candle from the pantry, and lit it. She pulled open the door to the basement.

Musty air drifted up to her, full of the odour of roots and water. The candle cast a halo as she clopped down the wooden steps, her hand on the rough brick wall. She bumped into a large crate at the base of the stairs.

After she rubbed her shin, she ran her fingers along the wooden top. What was it doing right next to the stairs?

She raised her candle above her head. The cellar lit up like a smuggler's cave, filled with dozens of crates pushed against the walls or stacked on the floor with just enough space between them to squeeze past.

She stumbled forward. "Oh, Edmund! What have you gotten yourself into?" She frowned. "And how did you get all this delivered without anybody noticing?"

Holding the candle high, she crept into the gloom. In the back of the cellar, light gleamed off a boom and tackle suspended from the ceiling.

"What the —." Rosemary stepped toward it.

Suddenly, she heard the distant jangle of the shop bell and the sound of Edmund's voice. "Rosemary?"

She whirled. The candle slipped from her fingers and snuffed on the damp floor. "Shoot!"

Edmund's footsteps clopped on the ceiling. Rosemary

stumbled toward the stairs and ran full-tilt into a crate, scraping her knee. She fell face first on the stairs. "Ow! Damn! Ow!" She clawed her way upstairs. She might just make it in time ...

She pulled open the basement door and stopped, staring. Edmund stood on the other side.

Rosemary brushed the dust from her shoulders and straightened her skirts. She smiled brightly. "Hi!"

Edmund's eyes narrowed. "What are you doing?"

Rosemary raised her eyebrows. "What?"

"You closed the shop," said Edmund. "Then I see you on the basement stairs. Explain yourself."

"Bathroom break?"

"On the basement stairs?"

"I got lost?"

Edmund pinched the bridge of his nose. "You saw the crates."

Rosemary folded her arms. "Yes, I did. So perhaps I'm not the one who should be explaining myself."

His eyes flared. "I rescue you from the street! I offer you room and board —"

"And you lied," Rosemary cut in. "You lied to Faith and you lied to me. I asked you if your business was in trouble, and you said everything was fine."

"Everything *is* fine," said Edmund.

"Smuggling goods is *not* fine," Rosemary shouted. "Those crates down there — Aldous made you take them, didn't he?"

Edmund didn't look her in the eye. "Yes, they're his contraband: goods and alcohol smuggled in past the tax collectors. It was either that or lose the shop."

"But to turn to a criminal —"

"I am not proud of what I've done! But Faith must still be put through school. She must have a roof over her head and food on the table until she can become a doctor! I did what needed to be done!"

"Do you have any idea where those goods came from?"

"No, and I do not want to know." He gripped the basement doorknob, blocking her path into the kitchen. "For your sake, you should not try to learn."

"Edmund, you are not sweeping this under the rug."

But Edmund didn't hear her. He was speaking to himself. "You canna stay here; that much is certain. Maybe ... maybe the church will take you. Peter is working; you could stay with the church until you can find your own place. Maybe ..."

"Edmund, you're not listening to me."

The front door jangled. Somebody shouted, "Mr. Watson? Are you in? Mr. Birge wants to see you."

Edmund winced. "Not again." He turned to her. His grip on the doorknob tightened. "You'll have to stay here."

"Edmund, listen to me!" Rosemary grabbed his arm, then gasped as he pushed her back. She staggered and fell against the landing wall, just catching herself before she tumbled down the stairs. She rushed the door, but Edmund pulled it closed. She piled up against it a second too late.

"Open this door!" she shouted, thumping on the wood. "Edmund, open up!"

"I am sorry, Rosemary." His reply was muffled. A key turned in the lock. "I ... I am sorry."

"Edmund!" She could hear his footsteps retreat to the hallway, then clop along above the basement ceiling. She would have followed, but there was no way she could see in the dark. She heard a muffled conversation, more footfalls, then the jangle of the front door, and finally silence.

Rosemary shook the door, but it held fast. She sank to the landing floor and put her head in her hands.

"That didn't go so well."

~~ :•: ~~

Both ends of the creek were now in sight. The southern tunnel had extended all but a hundred feet from the northern entrance, a sewer tunnel beneath Bloor Street. The icy mud of the construction site crumbled under dozens of feet hustling to meet the winter deadline.

Peter kept an eye out for signs of Rob's gang, but nobody stayed long on the hills around the site. Then Peter heard a conversation that made his ears prick up.

"Will Farley!" called Tom Proctor. "You're on diversion trench duty."

Will was a boy in his early teens, wearing shabby clothes and a cap. He stopped in his tracks. "Mr. Proctor! Why me? My feet will get wet!"

Diversion trench duty was wet work. The creek had to be dug out into a new course so that the storm sewer's floor could be laid.

Tom glared. "Because I saw you, Mr. Farley! Everyone hates the work, so everyone gets a turn. Now, who else?"

Peter raised his hand.

"See?" Tom shouted. "That's the type of worker I like to see!"

Peter ignored the glares burning holes in his back.

Moments later, he grimaced as the brackish water seeped over his laces. Will Farley struggled to wield his shovel and at the same time stand on a dry patch of land. He swore when he stepped firmly into a mud puddle.

"Trouble?" asked Peter conversationally.

"It's these darn boots," said Will. "Holes in the sole. The water goes clean through. Chills me to the bone!"

"Time for new boots, I guess."

"I *had* new boots," said Will bitterly. "But then I lost them. I had to stick with these."

Peter raised his eyebrows. "That's a shame."

"Ain't it, though," said Will. Then he looked up, and saw who he was talking to. His gaze darkened. "None of your business."

Peter kept digging.

Later, on break, Peter stepped close to Tom. "Tom, I need you to do me a favour."

"What is it?" Tom whittled away at a piece of wood. He did not look up.

"I need you to keep Will Farley behind a few minutes after shift before sending him on his way."

Tom stopped whittling. "What for?"

Peter smiled. "I just need to talk to him ... alone."

Tom looked up, frowning. "Be careful, Peter. Will's in with bad company."

"I guessed that," said Peter. "I think he was one of those people who attacked us that night."

"What?" Tom stood up. "Where is he? I'll throttle —"

Peter gripped his shoulders and shushed him. "That's what I want to talk to him about. I'll get him alone and make him confess."

Tom shook his head. "The police should be told."

"They will be," said Peter. "As soon as I have something to tell them."

Tom rubbed his chin, then nodded. "All right. But be careful!"

~~ :•: ~~

The crowds on College Street thinned as the sun set. Peter stood in the shadow of the Presbyterian church. He watched as the shadows lengthened and the lamplighters darted down the street, setting the gas lamps aglow.

The crowds were gone now. The wind picked up. Peter blew on his hands and glanced at the gaslights, half-expecting to see that strange phosphor glow.

Then he heard quick, booted footsteps on the wooden sidewalk. He peered out on the street and saw Will Farley, huddled and muttering beneath his breath, limping on bad boots.

Peter tensed, eyeing the distance. When Will was almost past him, he leapt into the light, grabbed him by the collar, and shoved him into the church wall.

"Hey! What? G'off!" Will choked as Peter pressed forearm to throat.

"Easy now," said Peter, smiling grimly. "Don't yell. I just want to talk to you."

Will glared up at him. "What about?"

"Actually, I want *you* to talk," said Peter. "I see you've been having a little problem with your boots."

"Yeah? What of it?"

Peter pressed down harder. "A few nights ago, Tom and I were attacked at the construction site. You know anything about that?"

"Yeah," snarled Will. "I heard the mates talk about it. Mr. Proctor weren't hurt, so what?"

"I wanted to report it to the police," said Peter. "He wouldn't let me. He said we didn't have enough evidence, though I was able to grab a boot off one attacker.

Size eight. Common enough, apparently. But here's the thing: you start complaining about old boots."

Will's eyes narrowed. He stayed silent.

Peter leaned back. "How about we go back and see if the shoe fits. If it doesn't, I apologize; if it does, we call the police. I think that's fair. So, really, the question is ...," he leaned forward, dropping his voice an octave, "do you feel lucky ... punk?"

Will blinked at him. "What?"

"Look, I know you were there, so answer me straight: what were you doing there?"

Will pushed away from the wall. "Yeah, I was there, but I weren't going for Mr. Proctor!"

"So, what were you doing, then?"

"Inspectin' for His Nibs."

That phrase again, thought Peter. "How did you get in?"

Will sneered. "The river tunnel."

"I knew it!" Peter punched the air. "You've got a network in there, don't you? You're using the sewers to smuggle things right under the noses of the police!"

Will chuckled. "Noses. Feet, too."

"Why are you so interested in the construction site?"

Will shrugged. "It's a link, i'nnit? When the tunnel's finished, we reach the north end of the city."

That explains the construction site, not the watches, thought Peter. Maybe "His Nibs" found more than he was looking for. "Last question: I think I know already, but I want you to spell it out. Who is this 'Nibs' character?"

Will shrugged. A smile touched his lips. "Dunno. Just me and my friends work for him and his friends."

Peter scowled at him. "Would your friends know him?"

Will grinned. "Ask."

Peter whirled around. Three young men surrounded him, fists raised. There were the two boys he'd gotten fired, and Rob Cameron. Rob's nose was out of the bandage at last, but was still purple and crooked.

Rob's teeth flashed in the twilight. "Stool pigeon?"

"Yeah," said Will. "Wants to see His Nibs."

"That can be arranged."

Peter lunged at Rob, knocking him down, but Will and one of the other boys tackled him. Then everybody was on him, punching and kicking. A boot caught his chin. He tasted blood, and that was all he knew for a while.

~~ :•: ~~

After Will had left, complaining loudly about having to re-stack a pile of bricks that had been mysteriously knocked down, Tom had casually brushed brick dust off his hands, closed the gate, and walked to his cabin and lit his lantern. Hoisting it, he stepped back out into the construction site and did his rounds, following the perimeter to ensure there were no gaps in the hoarding, no new way for thieves to sneak in and pilfer his materials.

At the north end of the site, he paused at the remnant of the river, now a carved trench holding a trickle of slimy water. The sides had been denuded of vegetation. The bare earth was bright in the setting sun. The two tunnel mouths gaped at each other, rushing to kiss at a hundred feet apart. Tom took a deep breath and sighed. Then he turned away to return to his hut.

A splash made him turn around.

He found himself staring back at the river, but it was just as he'd left it. There was no ripple on the surface, no shifting shadows that suggested intruders. After a moment of watchful silence, he turned away again.

He heard a singing of line, a light plosh, then a thrash of flailing water. Tom whirled around and looked about wildly.

He *knew* that sound. Someone was fishing. Someone had *caught* a fish! But as he peered through the deepening twilight, there was nothing but the two tunnels, and Taddle Creek's last dying breadth. More silence.

Hardly surprising, he told himself. Nobody had fished the Taddle for twenty years. Only a fool would try today.

But ...

As Tom watched, the water began to glow. The light stretched out along the short surface of the stream, and beyond. Tom followed the glow as it obscured the southern tunnel mouth, and he caught ghostly images within it. His mouth fell open as the glow filled the horizon.

Before him stretched an expanse of glowing green. Ghostly reeds waved in the wind. The air twittered with birdsong and hummed with the drone of lazy bees. Flowers and ferns furred the creek's banks, and there was the pond, water black with leaf tannin and smelling of autumn.

Then he heard the singing of line again, the light plosh, and he turned. Across Taddle Creek, a young man stood on the bank, swinging his fishing line into the water. He peered at the surface of the water and swung his line again. There was a pause of anticipation, then the line jerked. The young man laughed and hauled a trout to the surface.

Hoisting his trophy in triumph, the young man looked across the river at old Tom. Their eyes met. Tom stared back at a face that hadn't stared at him out of a mirror for thirty years.

The young man smiled and tipped his hat.

Tom burst out laughing. He waved back, then looked around at his glowing surroundings. He breathed it in deep. Then, with the exuberance of a schoolboy, Tom ran, following the ghostly river along its bank as the glow eased downstream.

~~ :•: ~~

Peter woke with a splitting headache and the feeling that something had crawled into his mouth and died. He tried to spit it out, but it wouldn't budge. Something was wrapped across his lips, forcing the vile thing in. He gagged and retched. His hands jerked uselessly. They were twisted behind him and cuffed together, tied to cuffs latched to his ankles. He grunted in pain.

Someone behind him chuckled. "'Ere, he's awake."

He opened his eyes, blinking at the sudden brightness. He was bound to a wooden chair in the middle of a small, lamplit room. Hammers, crowbars, and saws dangled from hooks and shelving. He was tied so tight that his feet didn't touch the floor. More ropes wound around his legs and chest. He struggled, but his wrists chafed. He grunted again.

Someone stepped around his chair and peered close. Peter found himself staring into the face of one of the boys he'd gotten fired. The boy sneered. "He's the one. A stool pigeon, too? I should have known. Well, I'll learn you ...." He raised his fist. Peter closed his eyes.

"That's enough," said a smooth, cultured voice. The boy glared, shrugged, then stalked away. Aldous Birge and Rob Cameron stepped around Peter's chair and leaned in. Aldous tested the ropes that were holding Peter taut. "Comfortable?"

Peter grunted.

Aldous glanced at Rob. "Recognize him?"

"No," said Rob, frowning. "But I know him from somewhere, I'm sure of it."

Aldous turned back to Peter. "Peter ... McAllister, is it? I'm Aldous Birge. It seems that you know who I am."

Peter grunted again.

Aldous crouched low, peering into Peter's eyes. "I have to say that your knowledge troubles me. I have prided myself on keeping a low profile where the police are concerned. It appears I may have underestimated their investigative skills."

Peter stared. Was Aldous interested in having him talk, or not?

Aldous started to say something more, but was interrupted by a knock from somewhere behind Peter. A door creaked open. "Edmund Watson to see you, sir."

Aldous straightened up. "Can't you see I'm busy?"

"Peter?" gasped another voice: Edmund's.

Aldous grabbed the back of Peter's chair and dragged it around. "You know this man?"

Edmund was flanked by henchmen. He stared at Peter like a man at a gaping chasm. He stammered. "He-he-he lives with us. He and his wife, Rosemary —"

Peter grunted desperately, shaking his head for silence, but he was too late.

"That's it!" Rob thumped his fist. "That wench who broke my nose! He was with her that day!"

"Rosemary?" Aldous repeated. "Rosemary Watson? Married to Peter with the last name McAllister?"

Edmund stood agog.

Aldous gripped Peter's shoulders hard. "You have been deceived, Edmund. Peter McAllister and Rosemary Watson, if those are their real names, have conspired to keep their true identities secret while they infiltrated your home and my construction site. Interesting that they knew where my interests lay." His voice ran like honey. "Or perhaps they didn't deceive you. Perhaps *you* have been deceiving *me*."

Edmund paled. He wagged his head desperately. "Mr. Birge, I assure you, I have no idea what you are talking about."

Aldous shrugged. "Perhaps if we spoke with your sister we could be more assured of your loyalty."

Edmund looked ready to faint. "No! Do not harm Faith! Please, Mr. Birge!"

Peter grunted, agreeing with Edmund.

"We will not harm your sister, Edmund," said Aldous. "But perhaps she will be interested in hearing the benefits of our business relationship. You can explain, can't you, Edmund?"

"Mr. Birge, please —"

"Bring her in, boys," said Aldous. Some of Aldous's thugs turned and strode out the door.

"And have Edmund wait comfortably in my office," Aldous went on. "Make sure he *waits*."

Two henchmen gripped Edmund's shoulders. Edmund gave Peter one more wide eyed glance before he was pulled from the room.

Aldous leaned into Peter's vision again. "I'm sure we can clear this up," he said. "I'll know better what to do when you tell me who you work for and how much you know. I'm sure you're interested in talking to me, just as I'm sure you're interested in rising from this chair."

He reached for Peter's gag, then hesitated. "But *I* am interested in the complete and unvarnished truth, and I think you might be more forthcoming with that truth after you've had some time to think over your predicament." He stood up. "We'll talk in the morning."

Peter grunted in alarm.

Aldous turned away, waving for his remaining men to follow. "Good night, Mr. McAllister."

Peter thrust against his bonds, grunting as the cuffs and ropes pinched. Will Farley, the last to leave, smiled and blew out the lantern. The door clicked shut and was bolted, leaving Peter alone in the dark.

CHAPTER NINE

~~ :•: ~~

RUN SILENT, RUN DEEP

Rosemary sat on the basement stairs. Enough light seeped in from under the door for her to barely make out the walls and floor around her, but the stairs vanished into a sea of darkness. She could have fetched the candle, she supposed, fumbling around in the dark for it, but without a match it was useless. She sat with her chin in her hands and sighed.

Then she perked up. How had Edmund delivered those crates unnoticed? Perhaps there were other stairs leading out of the basement. That would be worth fumbling around in the dark for.

Then she heard footsteps in the kitchen, and she abandoned the plan, leaping to her feet. Was this Edmund, coming back? "Edmund! Open this door!"

The footsteps halted.

"Edmund, please," said Rosemary, putting as much meek into her voice as it would hold. "Let me out! I'm just a helpless female and I promise I won't do anything to you." Under her breath she added, "Like kick you in a sensitive place!"

No response.

She thumped the door. "Edmund!"

The door swept open, knocking Rosemary back against the wall. She gathered herself for a leap, then stopped when she found herself staring up at Faith, who stood wide-eyed in astonishment.

Rosemary flashed a smile. "Hi, Faith!"

Faith pulled Rosemary into the kitchen. "Rosemary, what is going on? Did Edmund lock you in the base-ment?"

Rosemary hesitated. What could she say to Faith? Your brother's hooked up with a local criminal and he locked me away when he realized I'd found out? But her silence told almost as much.

Faith gaped. "Why did he ... Why would he ... Why?" Her face darkened. "What did you do?"

"Nothing!"

"Then why did he lock you in the basement?"

Rosemary brushed herself off. "I'm not sure I can tell you."

Faith grabbed her arm. "Tell me!"

Rosemary shook her off. "Edmund's fallen in with bad people! I found out, and he locked me in there until he could figure out a way to get me out of the house. There, satisfied?"

Faith stared. Then her eyes glazed. "The bolt of fabric." She turned away, her fingers twitching. Then she drew herself up and strode toward the hall door. Rosemary followed. "Faith?"

Faith pushed open the door to Edmund's bedroom and staggered at the sight of the mess. She shoved boxes aside and waded to Edmund's desk.

"It's locked," said Rosemary.

Faith pulled a set of keys from a pocket in her skirt. Selecting the right one, she slid it in the lock. It clicked. Faith pulled the drawer open and hauled out the leather-bound ledger. She flipped through it. Rosemary stood at the door, biting her lip.

Faith stopped and stared. She flipped between pages and stared again. "Rosemary, I am no businessman, but is not red ink bad?"

Rosemary nodded. "I'm sorry, Faith."

"He was losing ten dollars a month!" Faith stared at the ledger in shock. "Taxes were due, licence fees ...." She blinked. "But then he found fifty dollars."

Rosemary snatched the ledger. Her practised eye skipped down the line of numbers. "Found, nothing. He's been receiving ten dollars at the end of each week. It doesn't say from where; just like the first fifty dollars, which conveniently paid off creditors, taxes, and the licence fee."

Faith drooped. "Oh, Edmund, how could you?"

Rosemary touched Faith's shoulder. Then she paused.

"Where is Edmund, anyway?"

Faith frowned. "He was not here when I arrived ... Wait ... It is half past eight. Where is Peter?"

The colour drained from Rosemary's cheeks. She set the ledger down with a thump. "Peter?" She strode into the hallway. "He should have been here an hour ago!"

Faith grabbed her elbow. "What's that noise?"

They listened. A soft rattle of metal and wood came to their ears from the front of the store. The bell above the door tinkled softly.

"Edmund?" Faith started toward the store, but Rosemary grabbed her and pulled her back. They stood, watching and listening.

The store was full of shadows. The street light glared across the empty sidewalk and through the shop window. Two hunched figures showed outside the doorway. The handle twisted and the door shook.

"We are being robbed!" gasped Faith.

"No," said Rosemary, her face grim. "We're being kidnapped!" She grabbed Faith's wrist. "Come on! Out the back door!"

They walked quickly but quietly down the hallway and were halfway to the kitchen when they heard the door jangle and hard soles hit the storeroom floor.

"She's not here," said a gruff voice.

"'Course not," said another. "Check the kitchen. Check the bedroom." He gave a throaty chuckle. "Perhaps we'll surprise her in bed."

Rosemary pulled at Faith, who had frozen in indignation, and dragged her into the kitchen. She reached for the back door, but stopped when she saw the handle jiggle and turn. She turned to Faith and mouthed, "Did you lock the door?"

Wide-eyed, Faith shook her head.

Rosemary pointed at the stairs. Together they dashed, Rosemary heading for the basement, Faith for the sanctuary of her bedroom. Rosemary just managed to grab Faith's wrist and pull her to the basement landing when the back door opened.

A burly man strode in, turned, and saw Faith, framed in the landing doorway. "Faith Watson? A friend of Edmund wants to see you."

Hidden in the shadows, Rosemary gave Faith one last pull. The woman stumbled down the basement steps.

The burly man strode onto the landing and stared into the sea of darkness. He sucked his teeth. "Damn. Of all the places to hide."

"What's wrong?" said one of the voices from the front of the store. "That's where we were going to take her."

The first henchman stood out as a silhouette. He reached out and pulled the voice into view. Just the shadow of a head was visible. "Look down there. Did you remember to bring the lanterns?"

"I didn't. Smith did."

The silhouette flinched. "Smith? On the boat? You idiot!"

"What?" said the head shadow.

The silhouette's voice took on a lecturing tone. "Smith's on the boat. Lanterns are on the boat. We're up here. That," he thrust a finger at the dark basement, "is between us. You see the problem?"

The head shadow stared. "Oh. Right. Damn!"

"Get their lanterns," said the silhouette. "Or find their candles. Get me some light!"

There was a shuffle of feet and canisters. Something dropped and shattered. In the darkness, Faith let out a squeak.

Then someone let out a triumphant shout. "Candles! Found them!"

A match struck. Yellow light flickered. A candle appeared in the silhouette's hand. No longer a silhouette, he took two steps, stopped, and stared down at Rosemary, who had pressed herself against the stairs, looking up at him. Before he could shout, she lunged for his ankles.

The man fell back, knocking the other henchmen into the kitchen. The candle slipped from his fingers, through the slats of the stairs, and onto a crate. Faith snatched it up. Rosemary scrambled up over the man's body, her knee smashing his chin, and slammed the basement door closed before the others could rush. She leaned on it as they shook the handle and thumped.

She saw Faith standing at the foot of the stairs, holding the candle and staring. The first man sprawled between them, unconscious.

"Faith," she whispered. "Come on! Pull him up!"

Faith clambered up the stairs, passed the candle to Rosemary, and dragged the unconscious man the remaining feet to the landing. With Rosemary's help, they propped him against the door and braced his feet on the opposite wall.

Faith stepped back. "'Tis a very temporary solution."

"'Tis indeed," muttered Rosemary. "Is there any other way out of this basement?"

"No," gasped Faith.

Rosemary started. "Then how did they deliver all of those crates?" She slapped her forehead. "Of course! The boat!" She grabbed Faith's hand. "Come on!"

"Where are we going?" Faith clattered down the stairs after her.

"The other way out." Rosemary raised the candle and peered through the gloom until she spotted the boom and tackle in the corner.

Faith stared at the row upon row of crates. Her shoulders sagged. "Oh, Edmund!"

They stumbled through the aisles to the corner. Suddenly, their boot soles met hollow wood instead of foundation stone. Rosemary stepped back and shone the candlelight on a huge trap door lying beneath the boom and tackle. There was a smaller trap door within it, big enough for a person to fit through. Rosemary pulled the latch. Cool, moist air struck her face with the sound of running water. Stairs descended into the dark.

Suddenly, a voice called out. "Hey! Did you get her?" A light shone up and swept over Rosemary's knees.

Rosemary didn't drop the hatch. Instead, she blew out her candle and dropped her voice an octave. "Yeah. Come up here. We need help."

The man below chuckled. "Didn't come quietly, did she? Had to tie her up, did you?"

"Yeah," said Rosemary. "She's heavy."

"I'm coming up." There was a splash, then the sound of boots on wood. The lantern light shook as the boatman mounted the steps. He pushed the hatch aside and stared at Faith and Rosemary staring back at him. "You're not tied up. Where are the oth—"

Rosemary kicked him hard between the legs, doubling him over. Her next kick cracked his nose and he clutched at it. Her third kick struck his shoulder, sending him sprawling. There was a clatter of man on wood, followed by a splash.

"Rosemary!" gasped Faith, shocked. But her eyes gleamed in admiration.

The basement door burst open. The henchmen piled down the steps, candles held high.

Rosemary shoved Faith to the steps. They clambered down, and found themselves inside a long, square tunnel of running water. At the base of the steps was a wooden jetty, bobbing in the stream, and beside it a large flatbed boat, four feet wide and four times as long, bucking against the current. Two lanterns shone, one at the bow and one at the stern. They made the slick brick walls gleam as if molten. The air sopped their skin and smelled like all the alleyways in Toronto concentrated into a single drop, then multiplied.

The boatman lay unconscious, half in the stream. Above, voices and clattering crates approached the hatchway. Rosemary shoved Faith toward the boat. "In! Now!"

"What are you doing —"

"Don't argue! Go!" Rosemary pulled the rope from its hook and jumped onto the boat as it started to slide away. Faith gripped the sides, but it held steady under Rosemary's feet. There were poles on the bottom of the boat. Rosemary picked one up and pushed away from the wall, sending the boat toward the stronger middle current.

Then she looked up and quailed. The hatch was directly above her. One of the thugs stared down, a gun in his hand. He aimed.

"Down!" She dove on top of Faith, shielding her and making them both as small a target as possible.

The gunshot sent splinters flying. The tunnel rang like the inside of a drum.

Then the boat found the current and gathered speed downstream, leaving the jetty far behind.

~~ :•: ~~

For a long while, Faith and Rosemary lay huddled in the bottom of the boat, gasping. Finally, Faith pushed Rosemary aside and sat up. Rosemary checked herself for holes. She didn't find any.

"Are you all right?" she asked Faith.

Faith nodded, her cheeks pale in the lantern light. "Where are we?"

"Storm sewer," Rosemary replied.

They were in the centre of the stream. The wet walls curved above them, the brickwork sweeping past like picket fences by a highway.

Faith tried to gather her breath, with little success. "What ...," she breathed, then started again. "Who ...," another breath. "I cannot stop shaking."

Rosemary squeezed her shoulder. "I know." Her own throat was dry.

"What — what do we do now?"

Rosemary sat and stared at the passing brickwork. "I don't know," she said finally. "Get out of here. Find Peter and Edmund. I don't know where to start." Then her eyes focused. Ahead of them, the curved brick wall angled into what had previously been open tunnel. She shot a glance to her right. The distance between starboard and brick wall narrowed steadily. She stood up. "Steering! That's where we start!"

"What?" gasped Faith.

"Pass me that pole!" Rosemary snapped her fingers.

Then Faith saw the approaching bend and she looked around frantically. She found the pole lying on the bottom of the boat and picked it up. It was eight feet long and hard to handle, but Rosemary gripped it and dipped it into the water. The brick floor almost snatched it from her hands.

"I can't slow us down," she shouted over the rushing water. "Faith! Does this boat have a rudder?"

Faith turned. Stretching on her stomach, she reached for a twisting plank of wood resting beneath the back lantern. "Yes!"

"Turn it!" Rosemary's voice rose with anxiety.

Faith turned it. The boat lurched to the right.

"The other way!" Rosemary shrieked. Her words echoed throughout the tunnel.

Faith twisted the rudder, but it was too late. Rosemary threw herself to the wooden bottom as the boat smashed up against the wall, the starboard side rising as it scraped against the brickwork. Faith screamed. The boat slowed. Rosemary twisted her staff and planted the end of it against the wall. She pushed.

The boat eased back out into the stream.

Rosemary sat up and planted the pole in the bottom of the stream. It caught. At this speed, she was able to hold on, and the boat slowed, then stopped. She eased up and the boat started forward, until she planted the pole again. This way, she was able to keep the boat moving forward at a leisurely pace.

"Keep manning the rudder," she said, her voice steady. Her chest heaved.

"Yes," said Faith. She looked ahead. The boat floated forward in the murk.

Then Faith stirred. She looked down. She stood up. "Rosemary ... My skirts are wet."

"Huh?" Rosemary looked back, then down. Water sloshed over the bottom of the boat, edging up the sides. "We're sinking."

"What?" Faith's cry echoed through the sewer. "How?"

"The gunshot must have blown a hole in the boat," said Rosemary. "Running into the wall didn't help, either."

"I do not care how it happened," yelled Faith. "What are we going to do?"

"Hold us steady." Rosemary passed over the pole. Faith planted it in the water and held on for dear life. Rosemary clambered over the deck, searching, until she found an upwelling in the brackish water lining the bottom of the boat. She pressed her hand to it and felt a jagged hole in the wood. She cursed as her palm caught splinters. The viscous water seeped through her fingers.

"Rosemary, hurry!" Faith cried. "I cannot swim!"

"I'm trying!" Rosemary shouted. She looked around for something to stuff into the hole. Nothing could be seen. She pulled at the hem of her dress.

Then the boat vanished beneath them. Faith screamed and fell back. Rosemary gasped. The water swept over their legs. Crouched on all fours, Rosemary stared as the water rose to her elbows. Then the boat met the bottom with a crunch, and the water stopped rising. The lanterns dangled inches from the surface of the stream.

For a long moment, the only sound was the water lapping over their arms and legs. Finally, Rosemary got to her feet. "So, you can't swim. Can you stand up?"

"Do not mock me!" said Faith, bitterly.

"Sorry." Rosemary waded over and helped Faith to her feet. "Oh God, look at us." Their dresses were black, sagging from their shoulders. The weight of the sodden material made them stoop. "I'm afraid I ruined your nice new dress."

Faith stared at Rosemary in disbelief. Rosemary stared back. Her mouth quirked. Faith snorted, and then chuckled. Rosemary joined her.

Then the two were bursting with laughter, clutching each other, knee deep in the stream. The laughter lasted for several minutes before ebbing. Faith's chuckle ended with a sob. They clasped each other a moment longer. Finally, Faith looked up, her cheeks dry. "We have to leave this place. Now."

"I know." Rosemary waded carefully out of the boat. Her feet slipped on the brick, but she caught herself and helped Faith over. "Take a lantern. We'll walk downstream." She grabbed her own lantern off the bow. It was a storm lantern, ideal for ships at sea. The wick burned fiercely behind glass and the shutters were well-oiled and ready to click into place. The metal was hot to the touch, but the handle was cool.

"What if we find other boats?" said Faith. "Think, Rosemary: the jetty? The boat was waiting for us. This is not just a sewer, it's an underground canal."

"I know." Rosemary clasped Faith's wet hand. "But with those thugs behind us, we're stuck on this route, at least until we can find a way to the surface. We should have some time before word gets back that we've escaped and everybody comes looking for us. Come on."

They sloshed downstream, sticking as close to the wall as possible, where the water was shallowest. The lights from their lantern gleamed off the brick. The flowing water covered all other sound.

"Rosemary?" said Faith after a long while.

"What?"

"Why did ...," Faith began. Then she faltered. "How could ... How could Edmund have fallen in with those men?"

"You saw the ledgers," said Rosemary. "He was losing the shop."

"Yes, but ... Why did he not tell me?"

Rosemary shrugged. "He was too proud?" She scanned the ceiling for manholes, but found none. "He wanted so much to keep you in school."

"So this *is* my fault," Faith muttered.

"No." Rosemary turned on her. "It's not your fault that Edmund is the proud idiot he is."

Faith frowned. "How dare you speak of my brother like that!"

"How would you speak of your brother, then?" Rosemary shot back. She softened. "I know you love your brother. I like him too, even after he locked me in the basement. But for all that, he's still in over his head."

Faith bit her lip and stared at the water.

Rosemary squeezed her shoulder. "He's still a good man. He wanted me out of the house for my own sake as much as his. And when thugs try to kidnap somebody's sister, it's because the brother is having second thoughts about the whole thing."

Faith looked up. "Really?"

Rosemary smiled. "I bet you he's being held captive for his 'treachery,' and it's up to us to get the police and rescue him."

Faith gave her a small smile. Then she looked downstream and brightened. "I see light! I see the end of the tunnel!"

Rosemary turned. The tunnel flickered in the distance. A gleam of light pulled into view. Her heart leapt and she clicked the shutter closed on her lantern. "The light at the end of the tunnel's a boat."

"They've come for us!" Faith squeaked. "Run!"

"Wait!" Rosemary grabbed her wrist. The distant light set the bricks aglow, but there was a black gap, forward and to their right. The bricks on either side shone. "A branch tunnel! Come on! Quietly!"

They sloshed forward. Rosemary kept Faith's lantern light on the wall. Then they found themselves looking into a narrow drain emptying into the stream with a small waterfall. It was barely four feet wide and six feet high.

"Come on!" Rosemary tugged Faith toward the drain, but Faith held back.

"Rosemary, no." She drew a shaky breath. "I cannot go in there. This tunnel is bad enough, but that small hole —"

Rosemary pulled. "Come on, Faith! They'll be here in a minute!"

"Rosemary, please! I cannot!" Hysteria edged her voice higher. "I cannot take much more of this. The walls are closing in on me. I ... I cannot breathe!"

Rosemary shook her by the shoulders. "Faith!" She waited until Faith focused into her eyes, then continued calmly. "I know how you feel. I feel it, too. It's called claustrophobia. But you've got to keep calm. I can't be level-headed for the both of us."

"I cannot!" Faith sobbed.

"Yes, you can," said Rosemary firmly. "Come on. You're the one who's going to be a doctor. Think of all those men who laugh at you every time you enter the building. Are you going to cry in front of them? Would a doctor cry?"

"What about you?"

"Me?" said Rosemary lightly. "I'm going into bio-chemistry. We'll both be doctors, so we're both getting out of this!"

The light drew ever closer. They could see it bobbing on the surface of the water now. Rosemary tightened her grip on Faith's shoulder. "Faith, please!"

Holding each other's hand, they stepped over the small waterfall and into the hungry shadows. The small stream sloshed over their boots and swept at their sodden shirts. The slimy brick brushed their shoulders. They went as deep as they dared. Then, with a final glance behind, Faith slammed the shutter over her lantern. They pressed close and stared out at the main tunnel.

The bricks began to flicker with reflected light. Voices echoed through the tunnel, slowly becoming loud enough to make out.

"I'm sure I heard voices," said someone. There was a splash of an oar on water.

"Our company, probably," said another. "We're near the Watson jetty. You can ask them yourself what took them so long."

The long gondola and its three-man crew eased into view. The man at the bow peered ahead. "Didn't sound like men. Sounded more like women."

The man at the rudder chuckled. "Another one of Michael's sirens, perhaps?"

"Enough of that!" snapped the oarsman. "There are strange things in this sewer. I can hear them on the water. We shouldn't be down here, I tell you."

"You'd rather we try to sneak behind the constabulary's backs instead of beneath their feet?" said the bowman.

The oarsman muttered something surly.

The gondola slipped out of view. The watery light faded.

Rosemary heaved a sigh of relief. "They haven't started looking for us down here yet."

Faith said nothing. Rosemary could see her in the rising shadows of the departing lamplight, standing stock still, arms clenched around her chest.

Rosemary touched her arm. "Faith?"

She took a deep, shaky breath as the last of the light vanished. "We must leave this place. Now."

"We will." Rosemary gave her arm a squeeze. "We will, I promise. We'll find a manhole and we'll get ourselves out of here. Think of the open sky, the fresh air, our feet on muddy streets."

Faith chuckled. "I might take my boots off for that."

Rosemary eased Faith toward the river tunnel. In the dark, she reached out to use the brick wall as a guide. Then her fingers met open air and she toppled sideways with a shriek.

"Rosemary!" gasped Faith in a hoarse whisper. "Are you all right?"

"Yeah." Rosemary rolled onto her back, rubbing her bruised elbows. In a faint phosphor glow, she could see the bricks sweeping up around her in a small, thin tunnel. She patted the stone beneath her. "I'm on dry land. This branch has a branch and it's dry." Her fingers ran over a riser. She could barely make out the shapes ahead of her. "I think I'm at the base of a flight of stairs!"

"Stairs!" Faith rushed forward.

"Faith! Careful! There's a step —," but before she could finish, Faith tripped on the step, pitching forward and landing on top of Rosemary in a tangle of skirts and a clatter of lanterns.

When they disentangled themselves, Faith asked, "Are you hurt?"

"Just a little winded." Rosemary rubbed her stomach. "Can you give me some light?"

Faith eased open the shutter on the lantern. The shaft of light blinded them. They brought it round and shone it up a flight of cement stairs, topping out six steps above them before a battered wooden door.

"Freedom!" Faith clambered up the steps. Rosemary was hot on her heels. They tried the knob. It was stiff, but it was not locked. After a minute of rattling, Rosemary put her shoulder to the door and shoved it open.

Sunlight blinded them. Not waiting to see where they were, they stumbled through, catching themselves on a low wall topped by a metal railing. Rosemary had just the presence of mind not to let the door slam. She eased it shut behind her. She noticed that, on this side, it looked new, with a fresh coat of green paint. They leaned on the wall, blinking until their eyes adjusted to the light.

They were at the base of a small pit in the corner of a warehouse. Steps led up to a scuffed and dusty concrete floor that stretched to the distant brick walls. Near the ceiling, cracked windows — covered with green tarpaulin that glowed and snapped in the breeze like garbage bags — ran the length of the wall.

The floor was strewn with crates, some pristine, the rest broken into kindling. Footprints clambered throughout the dust, but the place echoed with emptiness. Somewhere a machine rumbled, shaking the floor and resonating in the women's chests. Somewhere closer outside, a hammer hacked away at echoing stone. The air was musty, touched with sulphur, but after the stench of the sewer it smelled as fresh as a mountain breeze.

Faith set down the lantern and leaned her forehead against the railing surrounding the pit. "Thank God we are free of that horrible place."

Rosemary stared around her at the wires that hung from the ceiling, ending in metal cowls: light sockets, empty and gaping. Machinery rumbled again. "Where are we?"

Faith looked up and around. "A warehouse. We may be in the factory district, south of Queen Street." She pointed at the light growing behind the windows. "'Tis morning. The factories have begun to work." To prove her point, machinery rumbled again. The hammer hacked away, louder than ever.

"Morning." Rosemary stared at the tarpaulin-covered windows. The sunlight shot brilliant beams through the swirling dust. "Were we really in there all night?"

Faith mounted the steps and strode onto the concrete floor. "We must not dally. We must fetch the constabulary and rescue Peter and Edmund." She spotted the exit across the floor and started for it.

Rosemary climbed up the stairs more slowly. She looked at the windows again. "Something's not right."

"Rosemary! Come on!" Faith was halfway across the floor.

Rosemary started after her, then froze. She looked back, her frown deepening. Then her gaze rose to the ceiling. The wires. The metal cowls. With gaping light sockets.

Electric light sockets.

"Oh my God, Faith!"

Faith had crossed the warehouse floor. She reached for the door handle. Rosemary ran for her. "Faith! Wait!"

Faith opened the door.

Sound hit her like sunlight. Cars screamed. Dump trucks rumbled. A passing tractor-trailer sounded its horn. There were jackhammers, power shovels, a piledriver in the distance. Faith clapped her hands over her ears and staggered down the building steps. The door slammed behind her.

Rosemary burst out after her and saw Faith standing on asphalt, staring about, stunned. An oncoming cement truck blared at her to move. "Faith!"

Rosemary ran onto the road, grabbed Faith, and hauled her back onto the sidewalk. The cement truck rumbled past.

"What —," Faith shouted like a man newly deaf. "What is this madness? What —"

"It's okay!" Rosemary held her. "It's all right."

"All right? All right?" Faith stared at her. "How can this be all right? Where are we?"

Rosemary stared across the street at a forest of rising buildings. The CN Tower speared up beyond them. She took a deep breath. "I'm home."

CHAPTER TEN

~~ :•: ~~

BETWEEN THE PRESENT
AND THE PAST

"Phone, phone, come on, I know the phone's been invented by now." Rosemary charged along the sidewalk, ignoring the stares of passersby, who stepped off the sidewalk to let her pass.

Faith ran after her, darting around the people, stumbling amongst the sights and sounds. "Rosemary please, slow down! How can this be your home? What is this place?"

"Toronto!"

They reached an intersection. Faith caught Rosemary's arm and pointed at the horseless carriages and the massive, rumbling streetcar. "This is not the city I live in!"

"I know." Rosemary bounced on the balls of her feet, drinking in the sights and sounds and smells of the city. She wrinkled her nose at the exhaust fumes. The smells she could do without. "I mean, this is where *I* came from, before I met you. We're in your future, and I have to call my parents."

"Rosemary ...." There was a rising edge to Faith's voice.

"Look," Rosemary snapped. "How hard is it, really, to believe? Why do you think we talk so funny? Why did our clothes look so strange when you found us? Why else did we have so much trouble understanding the value of your money? Isn't that the only explanation that makes sense?"

"But this is the stuff of Lewis Carroll!" Faith yelled. "Time travel? You cannot be serious!"

Rosemary gestured at a passing car. Across the street, passing youths whistled and jeered. Rosemary ignored them. Faith stared about, going pale.

Rosemary threw up her hands. "Think what you like. I have to phone home." The light turned and she started across the intersection.

Faith ran after her. "A telephone? Why?"

Rosemary closed her eyes. "Because it's been three months since I talked to my family. I don't even know how long it's been on this side of the portal. I have to tell them I'm all right. Now, either you help me find a phone, or stop asking me stupid questions!"

"Why would there be a phone out here?"

Rosemary growled in frustration.

"Well, I see a sign for one over there!" Faith squinted into the rising sun and pointed to a row of booths at the side of a building. Rosemary strode for it, but Faith held back. "They do not look like telephones."

Rosemary brushed past two businessmen who gaped at her and at Faith as they passed. One turned to the other with a shrug. "Carollers? Little early for Christmas."

She squeezed her skirts inside the battered and scratched booth, not the least bothered by the smell. She closed the door on the chilly wind and took a deep breath in the sudden, relative silence. Then she picked up the receiver.

She stared at the coin slot a long moment, shocked at the high price of phone calls. Then she remembered she wasn't dealing with 1880 quarters. Not that this meant much; she didn't have any quarters, and she didn't remember Theo's phone number.

That meant her parents, whom she could call collect.

She flicked the cradle and jabbed at the numbers.

Then she stopped, pressed the cradle, and stared at the LED screen as the time and date came up.

WELCOME TO BELL
08:35:15 11/15/08

November fifteenth. It had been late August when they'd helped Theo into his new apartment.

She hung up the phone and stood, her hand frozen halfway to her side. Then she reached for the phone, hesitated again, and plucked it from its cradle. Another hesitation. Then she started to dial.

"Thank you for choosing Bell Canada," chirped the automated attendant. "If this is a collect call, please press '1' now."

Rosemary pressed "1". The tone blared in her ear.

"At the sound of the tone, please state your name."

Beep!

"R-Rosemary," she croaked. "Rosemary Watson!"

"Thank you," said the computer voice. "Please stay on the line while I see if your party accepts the charges."

A phone rang at the other end of the line. Rosemary clenched the cord. Finally, someone picked up. "Kate Watson."

Rosemary gasped. "Mom!"

The automated attendant cut between them. "This is Bell Canada. You have a collect call from —"

Rosemary's recorded voice said, "R-Rosemary. Rosemary Watson!"

"To accept the charges, please press —"

There was an emphatic beep. The attendant disappeared.

"Rosemary?" Her mother's gasp was almost a scream. "Rosemary, is that you? Oh, thank God! Where are you?"

"Mom!" Rosemary gasped. Her eyes ran with tears and she cleared her nose with a sniff. "Mom, I'm in Toronto. I've missed you so much! I couldn't call. I —"

"It's okay." Her mother's voice shook with the effort to stay calm. "It's okay, my darling one. It's okay. But where did you go?"

"1884."

"What?"

"We fell through a hole in Theo's floor," Rosemary sobbed. "We wandered through these tunnels and came out back in time!" She gulped. "We had no money, no food. A family took us in, but then we got in trouble. Some smugglers chased us into the sewers, and we came through this door and here we are, nearly three months later. I've been gone so long, and Peter's in trouble and I'm scared. I've missed school, and you don't believe a word I'm saying because it's just too fantastic!"

"Shh, Rosemary, it's okay. Shh." Rosemary rocked to her mother's words. "It's okay, Rosemary, I believe you."

Rosemary sniffed. "You do?"

"Of course I do. A mom knows these things. And it's not like this is the first weird thing that's happened to us." Then her bravado cracked. "Oh, my darling, we searched those tunnels for weeks. The police said you were swept out to the lake. Theo was beside himself ...." She took a deep breath.

Tears welled up again. "I'm sorry, Mom! I'm so sorry!"

"Don't you go blaming yourself!" her mother snapped. "You're home now, and that's all that matters. Get yourself to the nearest police station, right now, and call me. Theo can pick you up; I'll tell him everything. I'll call Peter's uncle, too. We'll drive down immediately. We'll have you both back in Clarksbury before you know it!"

Rosemary's knuckles whitened on the phone. Her mother caught something in the silence. "Rosemary," she asked after a moment. "Peter *is* with you, isn't he?"

Rosemary looked up, and saw Faith, ragged, standing at the edge of the sidewalk with her arms wrapped around herself, flinching at the sound of a horn.

Then Rosemary caught the glint of her promise ring. She stared at it a long time. She didn't hear her mother until she called her name twice.

"Mom." She swallowed hard. "I've got to go back."

Silence stretched again.

"These portals," she continued, "they're temporary. We tried to go back through the hole we fell into, but the portal wasn't there. We never heard Theo calling us. This other portal could vanish at any moment. We were separated. Peter's still in there. I can't leave him."

"Rosemary." Her mother's voice was tight. "There has to be some other way, the police —"

"— would call the doctors the moment I mentioned time travel," Rosemary cut in.

"Theo, then. You can't go back in alone —"

"Mom —"

"Rosemary, please, I have to see you! I have to know you're all right. Surely you can wait —"

"How long did it take before Theo shouted after

us?" said Rosemary. "The portal must have vanished the moment we went through. We don't have time. Mom, you know I'm right."

There was more silence on the line. Then her mother whispered, "Yes."

"There are other portals," said Rosemary. "After I rescue Peter, I'll find one."

"Right!" Rosemary's mother took a deep breath. "When you get back to now, go straight to Theo's new address. They closed the apartments after the floor fell in, so he's at the Rochelle residence, 350 Bloor Street West, apartment 11C. You got that?"

"Rochelle residence, 350 Bloor Street West, apartment 11C. Got it!"

"You go get Peter and bring him back safe, you hear?"

"I will," said Rosemary. "I love you, Mom!"

"I love you too!" Her mother's voice quivered, but she ploughed on. "We'll wait for you, however long it takes. Come home soon."

"Goodbye, Mom." Rosemary hung up, then immediately grabbed back the receiver and held it for a long time. Then she shoved her way out the folding door and onto the street.

Faith turned, looking anxious, but at the sight of Rosemary's face she stepped forward and opened her arms. Rosemary cried onto her shoulder, ignoring the looks of passersby.

~~ :•: ~~

"Are you certain?" Faith rushed to keep up with Rose-mary as they strode back to the warehouse. "This is your home, your time! Don't you want to stay?"

"Of course I do!" Rosemary kept her puffy eyes fixed on the sidewalk ahead. People in business suits and briefcases sidestepped out of her way. "But I'm not leaving Peter behind."

"But to go back alone?" Faith persisted.

Rosemary rounded on her. "Who'd believe us? If we don't go back now, we might not be able to go back." She turned and continued, walking even faster.

"How do you know?" Faith trotted alongside. "How can these things even exist? And what do they have to do with Edmund and those horrible men?"

They reached the warehouse. Rosemary turned to the door and found herself staring at a sheet of plywood. She ran her hands along it.

"Rosemary?" Faith frowned at the plywood wall. "What happened?"

"What on earth are you two wearing?"

The two women turned. They found themselves staring at a tall, clean-shaven young man in a suit and tie, a cellphone forgotten in his hand. He glanced at the hoarding and nodded. "So, your bosses didn't let *you* know they'd cleared out either, eh?"

"Wh—?" stammered Rosemary.

"Look." The man jabbed his cellphone at them. "If you ever find your employers, tell them they made their last deal with Newman Imports. We had an agreement: three gross of unbreakable china plates in exchange for genuine Victorian furniture. You think we wouldn't notice you sent us replicas? Talk about insulting our intelligence. You didn't even try to make them look old!"

"But we —," Faith began.

"And another thing! You guys are *weird*, with your strange clothes and funny way of talking. It doesn't surprise me in the least to find this place boarded up. I've checked the records on this place. Did you know this building's condemned? Construction crews are lining up to demolish it as we speak. You guys are the weirdest fly-by-night operators I've ever encountered. Are your clothes some sort of gimmick or something? Well, whatever; if your bosses know what's good for them, they'd better not show their faces in our offices again, or there'll be hell to pay, got it? Goodbye!"

He snapped his cellphone shut, brushed past them, and strode down the street to his double-parked sports car, which opened with a beep at his approach.

Faith stared after him. Rosemary turned her attention back to the hoarding. "This must have gone up after we left the place. We've got to get in there."

"How?" said Faith.

"Tools? A crowbar?" Rosemary thumped the ply-wood. "We don't have time!" She pressed her forehead against the barrier and took a deep breath.

Then she caught a glimmer out of the corner of her eye. It reminded her of a blue glow, like St. Elmo's fire. But when she looked, she found herself staring at the empty entrance of an alleyway. She pushed away from the wall and stepped toward it slowly.

"Rosemary?" Faith followed.

Rosemary turned into the alleyway. It stretched ahead, empty, plywood barrier on one side, boarded-up brick on the other. Frowning, Rosemary turned to her right and looked up the alleyway sidelong. A glimmer brought her attention whipping around, and she stared at where the plywood hoarding ended, past the end of the building. She strode forward more confidently.

"Rosemary, where are we going?" asked Faith.

"Looking for another way in."

"How?"

They turned a corner and ran face first into another hoarding blocking the alleyway. Rosemary smacked the plywood, only to have it flap on loose nails. She pushed aside the plywood and pulled Faith through. They found themselves facing a scratched and rusted metal door. Rosemary shoved it open and they stumbled through.

The door slammed behind them, echoing through the warehouse, leaving only the muffled sound of machinery and the click and scuff of the women's footfalls as they crossed the open floor.

"What was that about?" asked Faith, still being led by the elbow. "That man, and those things he said."

"Edmund's business partner," said Rosemary. "Or, one of Edmund's business partner's business partners. Edmund doesn't know it, but he's trading in items from the future." She grinned. "Futures trading, you might say."

"But how could anyone make a profit out of that?"

"Unbreakable china plates? Watches that don't need winding?" Rosemary raised her voice above the rumbling machinery. "How much would that sell for in your time? And all paid for with a bunch of cheap furniture."

"What did he mean about the construction crews?" shouted Faith.

"What?" Rosemary yelled. The roar of engines buffeted their ears.

"I said, what did he mean about —"

Glass crashed. Masonry rained down. A long section of wall toppled in front of them, spraying brick at their feet. A huge stone ball on a chain sagged into the warehouse. The chain tightened, and the ball pulled back, knocking more bricks free. Rosemary and Faith choked on dust.

"We've got to get to the portal now!" Rosemary shouted. Faith was ahead of her, scrambling over mounds of brick. She followed, then looked up in horror. With a leap, she pounced on Faith and knocked her flat. The wrecking ball smashed in again and swung over their heads. Brick fragments scattered into the pit with the green-painted door.

"Go!" Rosemary shoved Faith ahead. Faith stumbled down the steps. Rosemary tried to follow, but tripped and fell. She looked back and saw her skirt caught on the jagged bricks. She tugged the hem of her dress free.

The wrecking ball pulled back a second time. Rosemary staggered to her feet, then stared.

The door, swinging shut after Faith, flickered in the dust cloud. Its fresh colour faded. Cracks appeared beneath a plank of wood someone had used to nail it shut. The past was closing with the door.

Rosemary ran, stumbling over the uneven ground. Sunlight hit her, followed by the wrecking ball's shadow. She jumped down the stairs to the landing and hesitated as the door faded old for a moment, and then turned new again. A fierce blue glow leaked around it. She snatched up the lantern they'd discarded when they arrived, pulled the door open, and jumped through. She started to pull it shut just as the wrecking ball struck.

The impact slammed the door into her and pitched her into Faith. The wood cracked. And then the noise cut out so completely, Rosemary wondered if she'd gone deaf.

They lay on the stone steps, gasping. Gradually, they began to hear the rasp of their breathing and the sound of running water.

"Faith," gasped Rosemary. "I dropped the lantern. Can you find it?"

Faith's hands scrabbled on the brick floor. There was a clink of metal. "Here it is."

Rosemary beckoned in the dark. "Give me some light. Let me see the door."

Faith fiddled with the shutter. They flinched at the sudden beam of light. She aimed it up the stairs at the door. Moments before, on this side, it had looked battered and ancient. Now it was brand new. And locked.

"What happened?" said Faith.

Rosemary took a deep breath. "The portal's gone."

They leaned against the walls. Faith was shivering so hard, the light shook. "What do we do now?"

Rosemary shrugged. "Look for another way out. One that isn't a portal to my time yet."

"This is hopeless!" Faith yelled. "Our choices are to remain trapped in this infernal maze or rise to the surface in a loud and blinding future!"

"Hey." Rosemary touched Faith's shoulder. "It's okay. We'll get out, in the right time and place. Besides, you'd like my time. Plenty of opportunities for women. We even had a woman prime minister!"

Faith's eyes widened. "Really?"

"Yeah! She only lasted a few months, but she won't be the last."

But Faith shook her head. "It's no use, Rosemary. Try as you might to lift my spirits, I'm trapped here, and I can hardly breathe. I cannot see how things could get worse!"

"Faith Watson!"

The loud, gruff voice cut through the watery babble and made the tunnel walls ring. "Faith Watson, we know you're in there! Mr. Birge wants to speak to you!"

Rosemary jabbed at the lantern. "Faith! Kill the light!"

"What?" Faith gasped.

"Turn it off! Blow it out! Just get it covered!"

Faith rattled the lantern shut. Darkness fell, and they saw another light play over the bricks of the adjoining tunnel.

"Don't try to hide," said the voice. "We've seen your light, so it's no use pretending!"

They stood in silence.

"Mr. Birge just wants to talk to you. Come now, Miss Watson, you can hardly like your hiding place. Would you rather be left here, alone in the dark?" He waited for a response. None came. "Fine, then! Rot, if you want to!"

More silence. An oar dipped in the water. The women held their breath.

The voice hardened. "Come on out, or we'll get you out."

Rosemary took a deep breath and squared her shoulders. Faith stared at her with mounting horror. "What are you doing?"

"I'm going to them," Rosemary whispered back. "All this talk and no mention of me. These guys don't know there are two of us, and they probably don't know what you look like. If they take me, you can find your way out and get the police!"

"Rosemary, please don't leave me here! It's hard enough as it is!"

"Don't keep us waiting!" shouted the voice. An oar splashed. The light on the wall intensified. "You'll only make it harder on yourself!"

"Faith!" Rosemary grabbed her shoulders. "In another minute, they'll have both of us. Now, it's your call: stay and get the police, or go with them. What will it be?"

Faith stared at the approaching light. She closed her eyes. "I'll stay. Take the lantern."

"But you'll be in the dark!"

"They know we have it. If you step out without it, they may become suspicious." She thrust it out. Rosemary stared at it, then took it reluctantly.

Faith gripped her shoulder. "Be careful. You have no idea what these men could do."

"I know." They hugged. "Good luck!"

A hand smacked wood. "Right, that's it. Lads! Bring her out. Don't be gentle!"

"Wait!" shouted Rosemary. The light hesitated. "I'm coming out!"

"Hurry up, then!"

Rosemary pulled away from Faith, stepped down the stairs, and splashed her way along the tunnel to the main stream. She stepped into the light, shielding her eyes from the glare.

"Faith Watson?"

Rosemary laughed. "Were you expecting someone else?"

The light turned aside. In the shadow behind it, she saw one of the flatbed boats draw near. The silhouette of the oarsman gestured to the empty cargo space. "Step aboard, my lady!"

Rosemary rolled her eyes. "Such a gentleman."

She gingerly stepped aboard and gathered her sodden skirts around her. The oarsman pushed away from the wall. A boy manning the rudder guided the boat into the current.

Rosemary looked back. In the dying light, she saw Faith peering out of the branch tunnel, her face pale, her lips tight with determination.

Then the boat eased into a curve and slipped away downstream.

CHAPTER ELEVEN

~~ :•: ~~

AT THE MOUTH OF
TADDLE CREEK

Rosemary sat on the cargo platform in the middle of the long boat. With her hands cupped over her knees and her back straight, she looked, despite her ruined dress, like the Queen of the Nile. The bricks swept past.

The shabbily dressed boy at the bow of the boat looked back at her. "I hear you gave our boys a lot of trouble."

She gave him a steely smile. "I'm very glad to hear that."

He looked her up and down. "There must be more to you than your dress and glasses."

"Maybe," said Rosemary airily. "Or maybe I just caught them by surprise."

"Glad you saw sense at last," grunted the oarsman. "Saved us having to go in after you. Saved you a lot of trouble."

Rosemary ignored him. Instead, she asked, "What's it like, driving these boats? It can't be pleasant. No sun, the smell ..."

"Never saw the sun much, anyways," grunted the oarsman. "As for the smell, maybe you never smelled the like, you with your Yonge Street store and your schoolin' at the edge of the city. Try to make a living in the back alleys and you'll see why punting a boat is better."

The tunnel widened steadily. They passed other tunnels, as large as their sewer had been under Edmund's basement, with jetties attached and some with boats moored. One boat was being loaded with boxes as they passed. Rosemary thought she caught sight of a Seiko logo, but it went by in a flash. They passed two other boats heading upstream.

"Why is this better?" asked Rosemary. "You're criminals, trapped in tunnels all day. When the police come for you, where will you run?"

"The police will never find us down here." The boy in the bow pointed at the ceiling. "Up there, on the surface, if you do nothing but sit on a church step all day, they'll lock you up for vagrancy. They'll tell you to find work where there ain't no work. And if you do find work, what do you get? Your back broken in a factory? A pittance selling papers to people who'd spit at you as soon as look at you? I'll take my chances with what His Nibs has found down here."

"And what has 'His Nibs' found down here?" asked Rosemary. "Don't you wonder how all this can be?"

"We don't get paid to ask questions," the oarsman growled. "But it's making him rich, and it'll make us rich if we stay long enough. You'll see. Around the next corner, you'll see."

They eased around a long bend, and Rosemary saw.

They arrived in a long, low, wide cavern supported by huge wooden beams. The stream ebbed, and the water grew rougher as the boat bucked against waves coming in from Lake Ontario. Rosemary stared across the jetties and the boats and saw the low horizon turning grey with the approaching dawn.

The mouth of the underground river had been converted into an underground port. Gaslights were fixed to the walls at the head of each dock and jetty. The place was a hive of boats waiting for other boats to dock. Men loaded and unloaded cargo. Other boats headed upstream, some laden, others empty. The sound of people working and speaking, calling out the distance left to dock, drowned out the slap of water. Voices echoed and rang across stone.

Rosemary saw a flash of light and heard a faint crackle-snap. She looked, and there was Aldous Birge, in his impeccable grey suit, standing at the outer end of an empty dock. Edmund's invention was in his hand and he flicked it like someone clicking a retractable pen.

"We found her!" shouted the oarsman as the boat

drew up to Aldous's dock. "We found Faith Watson!"

Rosemary bit her lip. She hoped Faith had found her way out of the sewer, now that the hunt for her was about to begin again.

~~ :•: ~~

Faith forced her way upstream along the small branch tunnel. The walls on either side were both a blessing and a curse, guiding her forward but reminding her how closed-in she was. She struggled to keep her breathing under control.

"I must keep going," she muttered. "I *will* keep going." She pictured the ruffian who had harassed her for walking into Trinity College. She pictured herself walking over him, crushing him into the mud with every step in a most unchristian manner.

She pressed on faster.

Reaching ahead, her fingers met brick. Brick on three sides. Her route was blocked. But how? Water gurgled over her boots. She felt down until, at waist height, she touched the rim of a smaller tunnel. To go forward, she would have to crawl.

"Oh my God," she gasped. "God, please, get me out of this place! I cannot go further!" Sobs shook her, and she stared upward, though all she could see was darkness.

Then she felt water drops on her cheeks. They were not tears. The drops fell from above, shockingly cold, and a gust of fresh air blew into her face. She felt around her and grasped an iron rung, and another above that, set into the wall. It was a ladder. Feeling carefully for footholds, she climbed up.

A round hole in the ceiling became a narrow tube. She continued climbing. Bricks brushed her on all sides and caught at her dress, but she kept going. This had to be the way out. Had to be.

Reaching up again, her knuckles struck cold iron. She felt upwards. Her escape was blocked by iron — a manhole cover, too heavy to budge. She saw light through a hole, deep blue against black. She beat against the cover and screamed.

Fingers fit through the holes and pulled. The cover lifted up and was dragged aside. Frosted air rushed in, filling Faith's nostrils — the sweetest breath she'd ever taken. A hand reached down to help her up.

She scrambled for freedom, putting her feet on a brick road, blinking at the gaslight and hearing the clatter of hoofbeats in the distance. She didn't care how forward it was: she flung her arms around her rescuer and burst into tears.

"My dear, my poor dear," said an elderly voice. Tom Proctor held her off at arm's length and gazed into her face. "How did you come to be in such a state?"

Around them, the gaslights went out. The poles glowed with St. Elmo's fire.

~~ :•: ~~

Rough hands grabbed Rosemary and hauled her to her feet. She shook them off and stepped gracefully onto the jetty. She stood tall as Aldous stared in amazement.

There was a commotion as two men leading a third burst through a wide set of doors and strode along the port wall to the jetty. They shoved the third man forward. Edmund trembled and stared at his feet. "I'm sorry, Faith," he gasped. "I'm sorry —"

Then he looked up and blinked at Rosemary, mouth agape.

"Hello, Edmund," said Rosemary. She smiled at one of the thugs. "Rob."

Rob Cameron glared at her. The bandage was off his nose, but a large bruise remained.

"Rosemary?" said Edmund at last.

"Faith's fine," said Rosemary. "She's still in the tunnels, but she's finding her way out."

"Thank you for telling me," said Aldous.

"I figured you'd guess that," said Rosemary.

"Indeed." Aldous turned and slapped Rob hard across the face. "You idiot! I tell you to bring me Faith Watson and you come back with the wrong woman?"

Rob held his cheek. "I wasn't on the search party!"

"Well, pass that on to the people responsible," Aldous snapped. "They're a disgrace!"

Rob seethed.

Aldous turned back to Rosemary. "Not that this is all bad. I wanted to talk to you eventually. Still, it is a shame to lose the other Miss Watson in the sewers."

"She'll find her way out," said Rosemary.

"She may find more than she bargained for."

"If you mean the time portals ... been there, done that!"

Aldous stepped back. "You know of the portals?"

"I'm from the portals," Rosemary replied. "Did you honestly think your actions would go unnoticed? We've been watching you for some time, Mr. Birge, and we're not going to tolerate your time crimes any longer." She winced mentally at the phrase "time crimes," but drove on. "This place is surrounded. One word from me and the time cops descend and throw you into a time prison. So, take my advice: let us all go, and promise not to interfere with time again, and we'll be lenient. Resist, and you'll face the might of our ...," she threw her arms wide, "ray guns!"

Aldous folded his arms. "Very well."

Rosemary blinked at him. "Very well?"

"It's a fair cop. I surrender." He grinned at her. "Call in your men."

"Um," said Rosemary. "We'd really rather not show ourselves if at all possible. I'd advise you to surrender first."

Aldous's grin widened.

"All right, I was bluffing!" Rosemary snapped. "But it's not like you could be so sure!"

"I do not discount my good fortune, Miss Watson," said Aldous. "I was as surprised by the portals as you were, but as my men explored, we quickly realized that we were the only ones who knew they existed. It was a perfect opportunity for profit, and so I came up with my brilliant trade scheme."

"Brilliant trade scheme?" Rosemary echoed. "You find a doorway into the future and you trade for trinkets? You didn't once think of going into a patent office, looking up the files, coming back, and inventing the paper clip or something and making a mint?"

Aldous looked away. "I did not think it proper to interfere with the future to such a degree."

"You just didn't think of it, did you?"

"Quiet!" Aldous snapped.

"And what about you?" Rosemary turned to Rob and the other boys on the jetty. "A man takes you into a world of light and noise and you just play along? Doesn't this seem just the least bit crazy?"

Rob shrugged. "I have seen many strange things, but Mr. Birge pays well. At least now I know where you got your ...," he chuckled, "'clothes' from the first time I saw you. A man could get used to the twenty-first century."

Rosemary rolled her eyes. "You wish." She turned her gaze on Edmund. "See what you've gotten yourself into?"

He shrank. "I'm sorry. I did not know what else to do."

"Coming clean and asking for help would have been smart."

Edmund slouched lower.

"I think you have distracted us enough, Miss Watson," Aldous cut in. "I wanted to bring Faith to ensure Edmund's loyalty. You interest me only as a potential threat. I wish to know how much you truly know of me, Miss Watson, and more importantly, who else you have told."

Rosemary folded her arms and stayed silent.

Aldous smirked. "If you do not tell me what I need to know, your husband — if indeed he is your husband — might be a little more forthcoming upon learning you are here."

Rosemary jerked up. "You have Peter? Where is he?"

"Safely stowed away. Or, just stowed away. His safety depends very much on how forthcoming you both are. Do you think you could loosen his tongue?"

Rosemary shook her head. "I won't help you."

"I thought as much," said Aldous. "You are very much alike." He nodded to the others. "Tie her up and take her to him."

The men pulled Rosemary's arms behind her and slapped metal cuffs around her wrists. She heard the click of the lock and gasped, then grunted as Rob shoved an oily rag into her mouth. She bit down on his fingers. He screamed.

"Let go! Let go!" he yelled, pulling with all his might. He punched her in the stomach, and Rosemary fell to her knees, choking. Rob clutched his bleeding fingers.

The men behind her wrapped a band of cloth over her mouth, tying the oily rag in place. Rosemary let out a muffled yell and struggled to her feet. One boy grabbed her, but she shook him off. He stumbled off the jetty and fell into the water.

Rosemary kicked as other hands grabbed her roughly.

"Restrain her!" Aldous shouted, stepping back from the fray.

Rob rushed in, yelling, then grunted as Edmund grabbed him from behind. The boy whirled around, flooring Edmund with a punch, then cried out as Rosemary kicked the back of his knee. He tripped over Edmund's body, falling face first into a wooden post supporting the pier.

Then somebody tackled Rosemary from behind and pinned her to the edge of the jetty. Her head and shoulders hung over the slapping water. She kept struggling.

Aldous crouched down beside her. "Drowning while gagged is a most ignominious way to die, Miss Watson. Resist any further and we will toss you in. And Peter after you."

Rosemary went still. They hauled her back onto the pier and left her lying there.

"I don't believe it," muttered Rob. He rolled onto his back and clutched his bleeding face. "She broke my nose *again!*"

Aldous hauled Edmund to his feet. "Foolish chivalry will get you nowhere, Edmund." To the others, he said, "Finish the job, then take her to her husband."

The other boys stood around her, nursing aches, cuts, and bruises. "You want us to carry her?"

Aldous thought a moment. "No. I can save you some trouble. Fetch the new chair." The boys brightened. Two of them left, chuckling, and passed through the freight doors into the bustle beyond. A moment later they returned, rolling a chair on casters. The others dragged Rosemary to her feet. She stared in astonishment.

"The future is most ingenious." Aldous took hold of the ergonomic office chair and displayed it with a flourish. "Never have I seen something as simple as a chair designed so expertly for comfort and flexibility. The wheels are a marvel, and even come with adjustable brakes. Perfect for moving yourself around ... or, in this case, for moving freight." He nodded to the others.

Rosemary squawked in protest, but the men lifted her into the chair, pulling her cuffed wrists behind the back and hooking them beneath a knob. They hitched up her skirts, pulled her ankles behind the chair's central leg, and cuffed them together. Ropes wound around both sets of cuffs and tightened until Rosemary squealed in pain. More ropes wound over her chest and legs and were knotted tight. Then everyone stepped back to view their handiwork.

Rosemary could hardly squirm. The ropes and cuffs chafed her. Her feet didn't touch the floor. The gag reduced her protests to grunts. She could only glare as Aldous smiled. The others chuckled with him, except Rob and Edmund. Then one of the boys stepped forward, adjusted one of the knobs, released the wheel brake, and wheeled her off the jetty toward the double freight doors. The others followed.

They pushed her into a warehouse that was more alive than the underground port. Crates were stacked on top of each other and people moved about, checking inventory against clipboards. Aldous directed his men to push Rosemary along the back wall, from shadow to shadow, out of sight of most eyes, toward a dark corridor lined with doors in the far corner of the floor.

They unlocked one of the doors and opened a dark room. One man turned up the gaslight. There was a grunt within, which rose to a squawk.

Rosemary looked up, and grunted in horror as she saw Peter, savagely gagged and bound to a straight-backed chair, looking back at her with wide eyes. He jerked against the ropes, shouting through the gag. It sounded like, "I'll talk!"

Rosemary tried to tell him to calm down, that it was all right, that *she* was all right. The gag mangled her words; the chafing ropes made them a flat-out lie.

They wheeled Rosemary in front of Peter, facing him, and set the brakes. Everyone stepped back.

"A tableau," said Aldous, chuckling. "All we need is Faith Watson to complete the picture."

Edmund held his head. "Mr. Birge, please —"

"Don't humiliate yourself further," said Aldous with a sigh. He motioned everyone to the door. "Leave them. We shall interrogate them in a few hours."

Rob stepped into Rosemary's vision, blood staining his mouth and chin. "Break my nose again, will you? I'll show you ...." He balled up his fist. Rosemary flinched.

"Rob," said Aldous sharply. "Come. Someone will see to your nose."

Rob glared, then relented. He shuffled out with the others, leaving Aldous behind.

Aldous cast one more glance at his prisoners, then he stepped over to Peter and undid the knot of his gag. "It is useless to cry for help, Mr. McAllister, but perhaps you could talk some sense into your wife. It may save you both some amount of suffering. We will see you in a few hours."

Then he left, closing the door behind him. Rosemary heard the lock click.

That, surely, was overkill.

CHAPTER TWELVE

~~ :•: ~~

A FIERY DEATH

Peter worked his jaw, spitting out his gag like a man eating spaghetti in reverse. It fell onto his lap and he gasped with relief. "Oh God! You won't believe how bad that tasted!"

Rosemary glared at him and grunted indignantly.

Peter grimaced. "Oh right. Sorry." He sighed bitterly. "I'm sorry I got you into this. This never would have happened if I hadn't been so stupid."

Rosemary shook her head and grunted to say it wasn't his fault, but he didn't listen.

"I just ... you were so happy, we finally had a way back home, and I wanted to help you so much, I must have gotten careless ..."

They had to get out, that much was certain. But how? Peter had been tied up for hours, and he wasn't even close to free. She was no different. The only thing that separated her and Peter was that her chair had wheels ... and knobs.

"... and I thought I'd just confront him. I should have realized he'd have his friends around ..."

She flexed her fingers. She could feel the knobs at the base of her seat. These adjusted things like chair height and angle, and released the brakes. If she could just reach them ...

The ropes and cuffs gave her almost no room to move. But she tried. She stretched for the knobs. She grunted and winced. Tears streamed as she fought her way downward, flexing her fingers, reaching ... touching ...

Peter stared at her in horror. "Rosemary? Rosemary! You're in pain! That's it, I'll give them whatever they want! Hey! Come back!"

Rosemary had two fingers on a knob. She let go and grunted at Peter for quiet, shaking her head.

"Hey! Get in here!"

Rosemary screamed through her gag. He stared at her. She strained to reach the knobs again.

"What are you doing?"

She growled at him.

"Okay, I'll wait."

She resumed her struggle. Her fingers touched one of the knobs again. Now she had all five fingers on it. Taking a firm hold, she pushed it, and the chair sank with a hiss. She gasped in relief. The ropes slackened, leaving grooves in her clothes that filled out slowly. Her toes touched the floor.

Peter grinned. "Good going, Rosemary!"

Rosemary felt herself grinning through her gag. She tested her slackened bonds. She had more movement, but not nearly enough. The cuffs around her wrists and ankles left her no hope of freedom without a key. And what was it about those cuffs? They made it hurt just to move her arms. Looking over her shoulder didn't help.

But Peter was tied up in a similar way. Perhaps they'd used the same cuffs on him. If she could have a look, she might find some weakness, some way to get out. She pressed her toes to the floor, pushed, and remembered the caster brakes.

Her fingers felt the row of knobs again. The loosened bonds gave her more room to stretch. The first lowered her seat, so the second ...

The chair rolled forward, running into Peter's knees with a bump.

"Ow," said Peter.

"H'orry," grunted Rosemary. She eased her chair around Peter, stopping with her boot when she was behind him. She reset the brakes and twisted herself to look at Peter's arms. She gasped through her gag.

"What are you looking for?" he asked.

Peter's wrists were ready to bleed, and no wonder: instead of two rings linked by a chain, his handcuffs were bands of iron that wound around both wrists like facing threes, hinged together and locked at one end. He'd scar if he stayed tied up any longer. Her own wrists ached in sympathy, or just ached.

Then she peered closer. The middle arms of the facing threes, which slipped between the wrists, didn't meet. Something could be shoved in that gap and the cuffs pried apart. But what could she use?

She eased around Peter and presented her back to him. She splayed her fingers to show her bound wrists. She grunted.

"What?"

She shook herself and grunted again.

He eyes widened. "Oh God, Rosemary, your hands —"

She gave him an exasperated muffled howl and tapped at the gap with her fingers. "Hi *he* ha?"

"Huh?"

Rosemary glared. "Hi *d'he* ha! Hi *d'he* ha!"

"Oh, ideas." Peter looked around their prison, then nodded at a corner. "There. Hanging on a hook off the metal shelf. A crowbar."

Rosemary swivelled around, spotted the shelf, swivelled back, and gave Peter a nod. She kicked herself across the floor in four tries, sized up her last length, aimed, and shoved herself into the shelf. There was a clatter. Tools dangled from their hooks.

She looked up in time to see the crowbar come off its nail. She grunted as it struck her shoulder and landed on her lap.

"Rosemary!" Peter cried.

She nodded that she was all right. She kicked and coasted back to Peter and sidled around him. Then she paused. The crowbar was on her lap and her hands were behind her. How was she going to pass the tool to Peter? She rocked her chair into his hands.

"Ow! Ow! Ow!" His fingers grabbed, but they couldn't grasp the crowbar. "This isn't working!"

Rosemary sighed. Maybe if she raised her chair an inch. Which was the knob for that? She fingered the row, pressed, then shrieked as the chair keeled over backwards. She and the crowbar clattered to the floor.

Peter strained to look behind him. "Rosemary! Speak to me!"

Rosemary groaned. The full weight of her chair and body pinched her arms to the floor and the crowbar rested on her chest. She looked down at it, then got an idea.

She tilted her body, slid the crowbar to the floor, then rolled the other way. On her side, she could move more easily — though more painfully — than she could when she was upright. She leaned back, grabbed the crowbar, and swung it into Peter's hands. He yelped, but caught it and held on.

Then Rosemary shoved her wrists around the dangling end of the crowbar, pressing it into the gap in the handcuffs. She could feel the metal scrape across her skin, slip between the two prongs of the cuffs, and catch. This will work, she told herself. "Hnow ... Heder ... Hol' highdt!"

"What?"

She rolled her eyes. "Hol' highdt! Hol' highdt! Hod id?"

The light dawned. "Hold tight! Got it." He clasped the crowbar tightly.

Rosemary braced her chair against a nearby table leg. "Hnow! Hull!"

Peter pulled. Rosemary squealed as the crowbar bit into her wrists and twisted her arms. Tears streamed down her cheeks.

Peter stopped. "Are you okay?"

Rosemary growled.

Peter took a firmer hold and pulled again.

Rosemary clamped her eyes shut against the pain, and pressed harder against the crowbar. The pressure increased until she thought her arms would break. She was about to beg for Peter to stop when she heard a crack and the sound of metal clattering in a far corner. The crowbar fell and the pressure eased from her wrists.

She shook her hands free and pulled them in front of her. She lay curled up, gasping with pain and relief.

"Did it work?" Peter struggled to see her. "Rosemary?"

She grunted for silence. Reaching up, she pulled at the gag. It took several minutes, but eventually she had it around her neck. She pulled the vile rag from her teeth and flexed her aching jaw. "I'm ... I'm okay. I'm still tied to this chair, but I have more options."

"Rosemary, I'm sorry, I —"

"First of all ...," Rosemary picked up the crowbar and grabbed the back of Peter's seat with it, dragging herself and her chair upright. "Stop apologizing. You weren't the only one who got us into this mess. Secondly, we're not even close to out of the woods, so shut up and help me untie you."

Peter struggled to hold his wrists out to her. "Oh God, yes. I've almost lost the feeling to my arms and legs. What's with this guy? Why leave us tied up for so long?"

"He's torturing us," said Rosemary. She slipped the crowbar between Peter's chafed and bleeding wrists. "Pretty effectively, I might add."

"Uh oh," said Peter.

She stopped. "What uh oh?"

"I can feel what you're doing. I think we're going to wish I was still gagged."

She patted his shoulder. "Bear up. I'll have these off you soon, then you'll feel much better. Ready?"

He took a deep breath. "Ready." Then he looked sharply at the door. "Someone's coming!"

Rosemary paled. "If they look in on us, they'll tie us back up again!"

The doorknob twisted. Rosemary tightened her grip on the crowbar and wheeled herself toward the door. "One chance. I hope this guy's alone!"

The door clicked, then slowly swung open. A figure sidled in, looked around, then cried out as Rosemary barrelled into him. He crashed into the wall and raised his hands. "Please! Do not hurt me!"

Rosemary lowered the crowbar. "Edmund?"

Edmund sat up, rubbing the back of his head. He stared at her in awe. "You're already out?"

"Hardly!" She rattled her cuffed ankles against the centre leg of the chair. "Are you going to help us?"

He pulled a key from his pocket. "I took this from Aldous's desk."

"He let you?" asked Peter in disbelief.

"They didn't see me. They think I'm still —"

She turned her seat around, holding out her ankles as far as possible. "Never mind how you got the key, hurry up and untie us!"

He fitted the key into the cuffs around Rosemary's ankles. Rosemary grunted as he pulled at them for leverage. Then the cuffs clicked and slipped off. She gasped in relief.

Edmund used a pocket knife to cut through the remaining bonds, then helped Rosemary out of her seat. She held on to him while her cramped legs protested. She looked into his eyes. "Thank you," she said. Then she slapped him.

He stared at her, holding his cheek. "What did you do that for?"

"For getting us into this mess in the first place." She

rolled her eyes at his hurt expression. "Come on! I'm glad you came to your senses, but what would you have done in my place?"

He drooped. "I'm sorry, Rosemary, I —"

"Shut up!" she snapped. "It's Peter's turn!"

"He isn't going to hit me as well, is he?"

"Just go!" She pushed Edmund toward Peter, then grabbed a shelf for support. Edmund knelt by his chair and got to work.

Peter gasped in pain and relief as the cuffs came off. The ropes took longer to saw through. Finally he was free and helped to his feet. The next moment he was on the floor, curled up in a ball. "Oh God! Oh God! Oh God!"

"What is it?" Rosemary grabbed at him.

Tears streamed down Peter's cheeks. "I've got cramps everywhere! I can't move!"

"He has been tied up too long," muttered Edmund.

"Come on, Peter, straighten up." She pulled him back to his feet. "We've got to get out of here!"

Peter tried to stand, but doubled over again. He fell back into the chair. "You'll have to leave me here."

She grabbed his arm. "No way."

"I can't walk," he gasped. "I can't —"

Then Rosemary took his face in her hands and planted a firm, long kiss on his lips that left him gasping. He gaped at her. "Why —?"

She stepped back. "To remind you of what you'll lose if you don't." She held out her hands.

"Oh," he said. "Right." He took her hand and grabbed Edmund's shoulder, using both to heave himself out of his seat. He winced, then took a deep breath. "Let's go. Slowly."

Supporting him as if he had two sprained ankles, Edmund and Rosemary led Peter out the door and into the dimly lit hallway. They shuffled to the entrance of the great hall and gazed out at the bustling warehouse.

"Are all those crates from the future?" asked Peter.

"You tell us, Edmund," said Rosemary.

He stared at her. "The future? You mean that insane conversation with Birge was not humouring a madman?"

Rosemary gave him a look. "What's in those crates, Edmund?"

He looked away, ashamed. "Tobacco. Spirits. Whatever it was Aldous stumbled upon, he wasn't looking for it. He is, first of all, a smuggler. He wanted to use the sewers as a means of shipping goods to the interior, beneath the feet of the tax inspectors."

"We thought so," said Peter. "That's why he's so interested in the burial of Taddle Creek."

Edmund nodded. "It provides him with the link he needs to the north. And my store was en route, the perfect halfway house."

"He's either the luckiest person in the world or we're the unluckiest," muttered Rosemary. "If Faith arrived now with a lot of policemen, would they find enough to nail Aldous for his crimes?"

"You mean, to indict him? Perhaps," said Edmund. "But look at the size of his operation. He must have ways of deflecting suspicion."

"And there's no guarantee that Faith is out of the sewer yet," said Rosemary. "So we have to find a way out." She nodded to a set of crates stacked by the wall. "We'll hide there. Go."

Keeping to the shadows, they tiptoed to the cover of the crates. Peter shook off their hands and used the boxes for support, limping along on both legs. "I'm getting better." Then he stifled a yell and tottered from foot to foot. "I'm getting worse! Pins and needles!"

Rosemary knelt and massaged Peter's legs. "Getting out is not going to be easy."

Edmund's eyes tracked along the warehouse floor. "It has just become harder. Aldous is heading for our storeroom."

Rosemary stood up. Peter turned around. All peered past the edge of the crate and saw Aldous, flanked by Rob (his nose bandaged again) and a group of other boys, striding forward purposefully.

Rosemary swallowed hard. "He doesn't look happy."

Aldous entered the hallway. Despite the presence of people moving boxes, the warehouse seemed to go quiet. The three glanced at each other. "Hide or run?" asked Peter.

Yells erupted from the hallway, followed by the scuffle of feet.

"Hide!" gasped Rosemary, and they ducked back into the shadows.

Aldous emerged from the hallway and stopped dead, holding back the tide of boys that ran into him. He scanned the warehouse floor. Rosemary watched him from behind the crates. There weren't that many places to hide, and Aldous knew it. She could see him checking off the less likely places: the part of the floor he'd walked down, other parts with too much open ground to cover. His gaze settled on her stack, and he strode toward it.

"Run!" She shooed Peter and Edmund out the other way.

They staggered into the open, past youths who almost dropped the boxes they were lifting in surprise, past others who just stood looking to anybody for guidance and finding none until Aldous shouted, "Seize them!"

Straight out of a B movie, Rosemary thought. But it did the trick. Men ran toward her. She knocked aside the first boy that grabbed at her. They were halfway across the floor, racing for the front door. Edmund dragged Peter along.

"Five dollars to the first man or boy who secures that woman and those two men!" Aldous bellowed, pointing.

Then the place came alive. Dozens of men and boys jumped up from behind crates, dropped boxes to the sound of breaking glass, and ran. Rosemary grabbed Peter for extra speed, but a circle converged on them. They kicked and punched, but there were too many.

Rosemary gasped as she was grabbed from behind. Peter and Edmund vanished beneath the melee. Rosemary fell to the floor. Bodies pressed on top of her. She curled up into a ball to protect herself from flailing limbs.

"Stop!" Aldous yelled, and the seething mass on top of them froze. "Get them on their feet."

Rough hands grabbed Rosemary under the shoulders and hauled her up. They set her beside Edmund and Peter, who looked battered and bruised.

Aldous marched up to Edmund and stood face to face with him. "When did you grow a backbone?"

Edmund drew himself up. "Much too late, I regret. I should never have helped you. I will not help you again."

"Fair enough," said Aldous. "Take them to the port."

They marched their prisoners across the warehouse floor and past the double doors into the underground port. There, they halted. Aldous nodded to the boy nearest him. "Order everybody out." The boy nodded and left. The port started to clear out.

Rosemary frowned. "What are you doing?"

Edmund tried to step forward. "Aldous, no, I'll do anything —"

Aldous pinched the bridge of his nose. "Edmund, I'm going to kill you anyway. It is better to die defiant than to expire snivelling."

Rosemary shot upright. "What?" She struggled against the restraining hands.

"I am sorry, Miss Watson," said Aldous. He nodded to another boy. "Fetch me a crate. We'll nail them in to drown."

"No!" Rosemary gasped. "Smuggling is one thing, but murder?"

"Sir," said the man holding Rosemary. "You can't —"

Rob shouldered him aside and grabbed Rosemary's arm. "I'll take things from here. You go tend to the warehouse."

"Why don't you just shoot us?" said Peter bitterly.

"Because the presence of bullet holes would leave the police no doubt that it was foul play," said Aldous. "As for why I am doing this, I'm afraid Faith Watson leaves me no choice."

Rosemary blinked, then broke into a grin. "She escaped, didn't she?"

"I appear to have miscalculated," said Aldous. "With Faith Watson trapped and soon to be captured, I thought I could interrogate you at my leisure, but my scouts confirm that she has left the sewers and has almost certainly gone to the police with quite a story to tell. My hope is to discredit her: to suggest that her story is the overwrought imagination of a woman whose mind has been broken by the tragic death of her family in a boating accident."

"You haven't actually met Faith before, have you?"

A boat docked at a nearby jetty and the oarsman

hopped out and came running over. "Mr. Birge, sir?"

He waved him off. "Can't you see I'm busy?"

Around them, the gaslights flickered. The bricks began to take on a phosphor glow.

Peter frowned. "What, the —"

"But sir," the young man persisted. "The northern drop points — the boys up there have done a runner. There's no sign of them or the merchandise we traded for." He stopped short, staring at Peter, Edmund, and Rosemary, lined up by the water's edge.

Rosemary took a deep breath. "The portal is flowing downstream!"

Rob shook her. "Be quiet."

"Don't hurt her!" Peter tried to strike out at Rob, but his captor pulled him back.

"Sir?" said the oarsman. "What's going on here?"

"None of your business!" Aldous snapped. He glared at Peter and Rosemary. "Stop struggling, you two! Don't make me gag you again, Miss Watson."

"Don't you see?" Rosemary's voice rang off the brick and gaslight. Heads rose. "Don't you understand? The gates are disappearing. Aldous has left all your friends trapped in the future!"

Faces blanched. Eyes shifted. Uncertainty rippled through the port.

Rob clapped a hand over Rosemary's mouth, then cried out as she bit him again. "Are you going to just stand there and let him kill us?" she yelled.

"Quiet!" Aldous shouted. "Rob, silence her!"

Rosemary choked as Rob wrapped an arm around her throat.

Aldous clenched his fist. He clicked his lighter faster, sparks flashing in the dim light. "What's taking that crate so long?" He turned and saw the warehouse doors standing open, a crowd of boys standing there, watching, blocking the way, arms folded. He glared at them. "Get back to work!"

They didn't move.

Aldous strode toward them. "I said, get back to work!"

Then a sound stopped them all. A low, echoing moan slipped across the water and resonated through the walls and jetties. The gaslights guttered. Some went out. A stagnant-smelling breeze ruffled their hair and caught at Rosemary's skirt.

"What was that?" muttered Edmund's captor.

"The wind, nothing more." Aldous rounded on the obstinate crowd. "What did I just tell you?"

The river moaned again. The sound was low at first, then rising until it wailed like a dying man. The phosphor glow slid downstream, seeping up the walls and shining off the jetties until everyone blinked against its brilliance.

"What is this madness?" Aldous growled.

Then the water started flowing backwards. The boys on the boats yelled and scrambled onto the jetties as the river sank and Lake Ontario flowed in. Wood clattered on sodden wood. Water slapped on stone.

Rosemary kicked back against Rob's knee. He yelled, then clutched at her, but Rosemary was fighting for her life and screaming at the top of her lungs. Peter struggled and struck back against the boy holding him. Edmund stared, then caught his staring captor unawares with a punch in the face.

A rumble drowned out whatever noise they made. The water shook. Around the corner of the tunnel, a giant wave rolled into view, filling the tunnel to the ceiling. The boys on the jetties rushed for the warehouse door, fighting their way through the shocked and panicking crowd. Edmund and his captor dove into the crowd for safety. Peter shoved his after them, then turned to Rosemary, who was still fighting with Rob.

Rosemary felled Rob with a punch and turned for the door. Peter grabbed her wrist, then fell when Rob tackled Rosemary, knocking her into him.

The water rushed toward them, smashing the first jetty to splinters.

Rosemary rolled around and kicked Rob in the face. He clutched his nose, yelling, and they were free. Peter hauled Rosemary to her feet, grabbed her hand, and ran for the warehouse door.

Behind them, Rob screamed.

They reached the door just as the wave hit. It knocked them into the warehouse and drove them to the floor. Water rushed over them, then receded. Peter and Rosemary, soaked, struggled up on their hands and knees, and stared. They were at the centre of a great, spreading puddle. Behind them was the sound of breaking wood as the port snapped.

~~ :•: ~~

A stunned silence descended on the warehouse. People picked themselves up.

"Is everybody all right?"

"Jim? Has anybody seen Jim?"

"What the hell happened?"

Then the front doors burst open, and a mass of constabulary came through the opening. "Right! This is a raid! Everybody stay where you arc!"

The crowd of boys broke in all directions. Some fell to the floor. Others looked for escape routes, and panicked when they found none.

"It's the cops!"

"We've got to get out of here!"

Still more ran at the officers, hands in the air, pointing behind them.

"I had nothing to do with it!"

"It were Mr. Birge! He was going to murder that young lady!"

"I saw everything, copper!"

The stream of officers filled the front part of the

warehouse. Gloved hands clapped on scruffy shoulders and hauled kicking lads out the door. Others fanned out into the crowd. "Come quietly, now. We'll take your statement at the station. Co-operate, and we'll be lenient."

Peter helped Rosemary to her feet, and then staggered when a policeman grabbed him by the shoulder. "Come on. You're coming with us."

"Hey!" yelled Rosemary, scrambling after them.

Peter gaped. "What are you —," he grunted as the officer hustled him into the crowd. Rosemary vanished from his view, blocked by the crowd of confusion. "Look, you've got it all wrong. I'm not with these people; I was their prisoner!"

"Tell it to the judge, son," said the officer.

"He's right. Let him go," said a woman's firm voice.

Faith stood in front of them, her dress stained and torn, her hands on her hips. The officer let go of Peter and tipped his hat to her before turning and darting back into the crowd.

"I see you've brought the cavalry," said Peter, trying to straighten his jacket.

Faith tilted her head at him. "No, I brought the police." She stopped short at the sight of his wrists and snatched them up. "Your hands! They're hurt!"

Peter tried to shrug. "They'll heal."

"Not without proper care!"

"Never mind that now." He snatched his hands away. "Where's Edmund? Where's Rosemary?"

Faith scanned the crowd, then perked up. "Edmund!" She ran to where another officer was hauling Edmund away. "Officer, wait! That's my brother!"

She slipped, catching herself on a fallen crate. She stood staring at the contents, which had burst out and spilled over the floor. The brown puddle reeked of alcohol. She rounded on her brother. "Edmund!"

He looked up, flinched, and looked beseechingly at the officer, but Faith grabbed his arm. "Edmund! Do you mean to tell me that you took up with ... with ... bootleggers and rum-runners?" She balled her fist.

Edmund cringed. "Faith, I ... I —"

"You stupid, stupid, stupid man!" She thumped his chest and shoulders. "How could you? How could ... You could have been killed!" And she broke down, sobbing. Edmund caught her, patting her awkwardly on the shoulder.

Peter approached, but kept a respectful distance. Then an officer touched his arm. "Since Miss Watson is occupied, I'll tell you. We have control of this place. There's plenty of evidence and plenty of people willing to point the finger at Mr. Birge. Tell Miss Watson she's earned a substantial reward for breaking this smuggling operation."

"Have you found Aldous Birge?" asked Peter.

"Peter!" Rosemary's shout cut through the hubbub. Peter snapped up and stared in horror at Rosemary being dragged back toward the river port by Aldous, a gun to her throat.

"If anybody follows me," Aldous bellowed. "I will shoot this young lady."

She clawed at the arm around her neck. "Don't just stand there, you idiots! Arrest him!"

The crowd of boys and police officers parted as Aldous dragged Rosemary to the port doors.

Peter ran through the crowd after them.

~~ :•: ~~

Aldous dragged Rosemary across the threshold and slammed the port doors shut. As he bolted them, Rosemary pulled free.

The port walls dripped and the floor was strewn with splinters. The river was crusted with the remains of boats and jetties. Everything sparkled in the rising sunlight.

Rosemary backed away as Aldous rounded on her.

"Do you honestly think that's going to hold them for long?" she snapped. With one eye, she scanned the floor for large planks — anything that could be used as a weapon. "Do you honestly think you're going to get away?"

"I have an escape route." Aldous nodded at the river tunnel behind him. "I have money stored away. And, for now, I have you." He waved to the water with his gun. "Find me a boat and get aboard."

Rosemary coughed and took a deep breath. "I won't be your hostage."

Aldous aimed his gun at her. "You will do as I say."

She coughed again, and held her chest. "Or you'll what? Shoot me with Edmund's barbecue lighter?"

Aldous lowered the gun. He squeezed the trigger as it hit his side. The barrel cracked and flashed. "I don't need a weapon to kill you." He started forward, his fingers flexing the trigger. Edmund's invention sparked.

Rosemary suddenly felt faint. She stepped back and swooned. She could hardly take a breath. The air smelled so bad ...

Then she heard the hiss over the slosh of water, the smack of wood, and the crackle of Edmund's invention. She looked up.

All the gaslights were out, flames snuffed by the wall of water, but gas was spewing into the underground port; it had been spewing for several minutes, now. Lighter sparking and flashing, Aldous was striding toward her, heading straight beneath one of the jets.

Rosemary leapt into the wood-strewn water.

CHAPTER THIRTEEN

~~ :•: ~~

NO FUTURE

Peter had just cleared the crowd and was running for the port doors when the explosion knocked him off his feet. He scrambled up and stared at the roaring flames. "Rosemary!"

Edmund caught him before he could run into the fire. "You cannot go in there! 'Tis an inferno!"

The crates nearest the port doors caught. Flames licked up the walls to the rafters.

"The alcohol!" the lead officer shouted. "This place will catch in seconds! Out! Everybody out!"

Peter struggled and beat at Edmund's restraining arms. "Rosemary!"

"Faith!" cried Edmund. "Help me!"

Faith grabbed Peter's arm. "Peter, please. There's nothing you can do!"

Yelling, Peter struck forward. Edmund and Faith

wrapped their arms around him and dragged him into the crowds streaming out of the building.

~~ :•: ~~

Rosemary sank into the murk as the air above her turned a brilliant orange-red. The explosion shook the water and echoed in her chest. She looked up at a fiery glow as the air ran out and her lungs began to ache. Then she knew she had to surface.

The air above was a mass of flames, licking around the floating wood. The water warmed by the second.

She pushed herself upward, but something tugged at her dress, pulling her down. She looked, but her legs were lost in the murk. She struggled to rise higher, but only drifted sideways. Bubbles of panic seeped from her lips.

Then she rose as though pushed from below, directly toward a black square in the yellow-orange sky. She burst into air and banged her head on wood.

She was beneath an upturned gondola. She could feel the scorching heat radiate off the wood. The boat itself was on fire, but she was shielded. She could take her breath. She could plan her next move. She sucked in air. She dove.

The invisible hands of the current grabbed her again, pulling her under. She brushed submerged posts, slipped over a garbage-strewn floor, until the sky above her turned from fiery orange to blue. The current released her and she shot up at the surface.

She burst out into the cold air, gasping. Lake Ontario clamped onto her like an icy hand. There was a dock five feet from her, and she struggled toward it, almost sinking before she managed to grab a ladder's rung. Then she hauled herself out of the water and lay gasping on the pier while a circle of port workers stared down at her.

~~ :•: ~~

Edmund and Faith dragged Peter screaming from the warehouse and onto the brick-paved street. Bells were ringing throughout the neighbourhood. The police cordoned off the road and held the crowds back as water tanks pulled by horses trundled into view, even as black smoke chimneyed into the sky.

Peter beat back blindly. "Let me go! She's still in there!" A stray punch knocked Edmund aside.

Faith grabbed him around the chest. "You listen to me!" Her breath fogged on his cheek. "Rosemary will not thank you for reckless heroics, so get a hold of yourself!"

He stuttered to a halt, then sank down to the curb. He hung his head and began to cry.

Faith squeezed his shoulders. "I am sorry, Peter." Her voice shook. "I'm so sorry."

Edmund crouched by Peter's side. He patted Peter's shoulder awkwardly. "I'm sorry too, son."

"She's all right," whispered Tom Proctor's voice into Peter's ear.

Peter blinked. "What?"

"Peter?" They looked up. Wrapped in blankets and shivering, Rosemary stood behind them.

"Rosemary!" Peter turned so fast, Faith was sent staggering. He clamped his arms around Rosemary in a spray of water and kissed her fervently on the lips.

After a moment, she gasped into his ear. "I ... can't ... breathe!"

"Sorry." Peter loosed his grip, but still held her. "I love you!"

"I love you, too!"

"You could really use a bath."

"We all could."

Faith sidled in and hugged Rosemary. "You made it!"

"Thanks to you," said Rosemary. "How did you get out of the sewers?"

"Mr. Proctor helped me," said Faith. "The foreman at Peter's work site." She peered around. "Where is Mr. Proctor? I thought he was here. There is something odd about him."

Rosemary noticed Edmund standing awkwardly away and reached for him. He accepted her hand, then grunted as Rosemary embraced him. "Thank you for rescuing us."

"But I —," he stammered.

"You rescued us," said Rosemary. "That's what's important."

"How did you get out of there?" asked Faith.

"I jumped into the river before Aldous blew himself up," said Rosemary. "It ...," she faltered, uncertain. "It guided me to safety, right out to the lake."

"The current guided you, you mean?" asked Peter.

"No." She frowned at him. "The river."

A police officer approached and called Faith over. After he spoke with her, she came back. "They are finished here. They will take our statements later, but they have offered to drive us home."

"Yes," Rosemary breathed. "Let's go home."

"I will run each of us a bath," said Faith. "Then a long sleep, I think."

Policemen guided them toward a waiting Hansom cab as the crowds dispersed, and Aldous's warehouse smouldered.

But Peter stopped short. He heard Tom's voice call to him. He turned.

In the dimness of an alleyway, Tom Proctor stood, smiling. Though he was facing the rising sun, he was backlit by a phosphorous blue glow, like river gas.

Tom raised his hand in farewell.

The sun slipped out from a cloud. Peter blinked, and Tom was gone.

~~ :•: ~~

The next day, Peter awoke with Rosemary snuggled beside him, snoring. They'd spent part of yesterday resting and recovering, but something gnawed at the back of Peter's mind: the raging river and the strange blue glow. He pieced together all of the elements and the strange sense of foreboding that had stayed with him since Tom raised his hand in farewell.

Then it clicked. He knew what he had to do.

He slipped out of bed, dressed quickly, and tiptoed out of the house. He strode through the waking streets. Wisps of snow curled around his feet.

At the construction site, the hoarding was half dismantled. Where the river had been was just a stretch of new ground. A worker shovelled in the last heap of dirt and tamped it down.

Peter walked down to the work site. A tall, thin young man in work clothes saw him and ambled up. "Can I help you?"

"I'm Peter. Peter McAllister?"

The young man brightened. "Ah, McAllister! I'm Albert Smith. I have your final pay and a letter of commendation from Mr. Proctor in the office."

Peter stared at him. "Letter of commendation? For me?"

"Yes," said Albert. "He spoke very highly of you."

"Where is he?"

Albert shrugged. "Retired, I guess. Didn't really elaborate in his notice. Some of the boys say he went to live with his son in Kingston."

"Or maybe he headed north," muttered Peter.

"Maybe," said Albert. "He was an odd fellow; he was a renowned foreman, but he tended to stick close to the university. Some say he loved the scenery more than the work. When it came to covering the river, he demanded the job. If it was to be done, it would be him that would do it, I guess. He loved the campus. It'll be strange not to have him around. Just like it will be strange not to have the old creek around."

"Yeah," said Peter, staring at the line of tamped-down earth that ran serpentine along the ground where the Taddle used to be.

"You know," said Albert, "a recommendation from Mr. Proctor carries some weight, particularly with me. When next year's jobs start, perhaps you'll join my crew?"

Peter looked up and nodded. "I'll think about it."

Albert gave him a firm look. "My next job will be a new building at the corner of College and Spadina. The university needs the space. Show up in the spring and you've got work, okay?"

Peter smiled at him. "Okay."

~~ :•: ~~

Peter strode back from the construction site, his fingers twitching. What was he going to tell Rosemary?

He found Rosemary dressed, sitting at the foot of their bed, pulling on her boots. She smiled when she saw him. "Faith tells me that the boots are supposed to be among the first things you put on. I never remember that."

"Rosemary ...." His throat went dry. He knelt before her and took her hand as she stared down at him. "I've got bad news."

Her eyes widened.

He took a deep breath. "They've finished work at the construction site. Taddle Creek has been completely buried."

She stared at him.

"Something tells me we can't go home anymore."

She patted his hand. "I know."

"You do?"

She took a deep breath. "When Faith and I were trapped in the sewers, we found another portal downstream. It took us back to the present. I got to call my mom."

Peter jerked back. "You what?"

"It was November. We'd been missing three months," she continued. "The portal through Theo's floor closed almost the minute after we fell through it. They spent weeks looking for us. I think the portal's been flowing downstream with the river. And when that weird thing happened with the water coming into the port? It felt like a door being closed."

Peter gaped at her. "Rosemary, you made it back home? You *talked* to your mother?"

She nodded.

"What on Earth possessed you to come back here?"

She looked at him. A corner of her mouth quirked up.

Peter smiled. "Oh."

They sat a long moment, staring at the floor, the ceiling, the bedspread. Then Peter looked up and caught Rosemary's attention with a squeeze of her hands. "Rosemary ... Will ... Will you ... Will you marry me?"

Rosemary stared silently for a long time. Then she said, "Yeah. Okay."

They embraced, and were quite late coming down for breakfast.

CHAPTER FOURTEEN

~~ :•: ~~

CHRISTMAS EVE

Rosemary noted, not for the first time, that without the privacy screens around the tub, their apartment looked much bigger. Snow drifted on the windowsill and the wood stove glowed.

Peter stepped in behind her, holding a stack of four glasses. Faith followed with a glass pitcher of eggnog. Edmund slouched in behind. "Why are we having eggnog in your apartment?"

"To thank you for acting as witnesses," said Rosemary.

"'Tis nothing," said Edmund.

"'Tis hardly nothing!" Faith slapped her brother's arm. "It was an honour, and it was a beautiful ceremony."

Edmund rolled his eyes. "We could hardly have allowed them to continue to live in sin."

Faith poured out glasses, which Peter passed to Edmund, then to Rosemary. "It was still an honour. And as they explained, Edmund ...," she looked hard at her brother, "they were *not* living in sin."

"Much," muttered Rosemary. She raised her glass. "We honour our hosts. To Faith and Edmund, great Samaritans both."

"To Mr. and Mrs. Watson-McAllister," said Faith. "Good friends."

"To all of us," said Peter. Glasses clinked.

Then Rosemary picked up an envelope from the bed and held it out to Edmund. "And we're here to give you your Christmas present. It's a little early, but here you go."

Edmund stared at the envelope. His eyes narrowed at Faith and Peter's grins. "What is it?"

"Open it, foolish brother, and see!" Faith snatched the envelope and pressed it into his hand.

Setting his glass of eggnog aside, he ripped open the envelope, pulling out a thick sheaf of papers. He stared at the covering letter. "My invention! I've secured a patent! But how?"

"That day you tossed your papers in the garbage?" said Rosemary. Edmund flushed. "I fished them out and finished them off for you. I thought, since you were no longer interested, I'd give them a try. I hope you don't mind that I forged your signature."

Edmund stared at her over the patent papers.

"I've done some legwork for you." Rosemary tapped the back of the sheaf. "Seems Mr. Ballard knows someone by the name of Mr. Bell. He's spoken enthusiastically about your find and he expects Mr. Bell will be writing soon, asking for a demonstration. He may ask to buy your patent. He'll drive a hard bargain, but hold your ground. Trust me, he can afford to pay you handsomely."

Edmund's mouth moved but no words came out. Finally he managed, "Rosemary — I don't know what to say. What does this all mean?"

"It means," said Peter, "that if you play your cards right, you won't have to be a pawnshop owner."

"'Thank you' should suffice," Faith added.

"Thank you! Thank you!" Edmund gabbled. He threw his arms around Rosemary, then let go, red-faced.

Rosemary held on. "You're welcome!"

He pulled back, still blinking. "I must get things ready. A demonstration? It must be flawless!" Mumbling to himself, he darted from the room.

"Merry Christmas!" Rosemary called after him.

"He'll be up all night," said Faith. "He'll be exhausted in the morning. Happy, but exhausted. I shall have to take care of him."

"Don't forget your studies," said Rosemary. "A new term begins in a couple of weeks."

"I won't," said Faith. "I had best turn in. Merry Christmas, both." She gave each of them warm kisses on their cheeks. "And," she added with a sly smile, "congratulations." She slipped out the door.

Peter and Rosemary faced each other. Rosemary took a sip of her eggnog and watched Peter over the rim of the glass. He reddened and looked at the floor.

"This is good eggnog." She took another sip. "Faith's recipe?"

"Mostly. I added some rum when she wasn't looking."

"Peter! If Faith finds out, she'll kill you!"

He grinned. "I don't see how she could complain. It's traditional."

She smiled sadly. "Yes, it is."

"Missing your family?"

She nodded. "But I have family here, at least." She looked up at him.

Peter took a deep breath and raised his glass. "Well, to us, whatever happens."

"To us." Their glasses clinked. Each took a sip. Then they kissed each other warmly. They had barely pulled back when they leaned in again. And again.

They stopped, breathing heavily. Peter's throat was dry. "So ... What do we do now?"

Smiling, Rosemary set aside her drink. She took Peter's drink and set it next to hers. Then she clasped his hands and stepped back, tugging playfully.

Peter grinned, and followed her.

~~ :•: ~~

Rosemary dreamed she lay submerged in water, gazing up as the last hole of light was bricked over. She reached for it, full of longing and regret, but she couldn't see her hands anymore. She clasped them to her chest and drifted off, as though to sleep.

She felt the current tugging at her feet, herself slipping through the dark tunnels. Then light began to glow, rising from her ankles. She tried to look toward it, but she was sluggish and lethargic. The light rose above her, and she felt herself surrounded in welcoming warmth, just as she faded from existence.

She slipped awake. The faint early morning light was just bringing shadows out of darkness. She blinked once, and took a deep breath. "Of course."

She slipped out of bed and wrapped herself in one of the quilts. She shook Peter awake.

He snorted. "What? What are you —," he yelped as she yanked the covers away. "Hey, it's cold!"

She let the quilt drop and started pulling clothes from the chest of drawers. "Get dressed and pack."

"What?"

Rosemary tossed over some trousers and began wrapping a couple of small keepsakes in a blouse. "Take a change of clothes with you. I know where the last portal is."

Peter rolled out of bed and got dressed.

~~ :•: ~~

Minutes later they sidled into the hallway, each dressed and carrying a bundle of clothing. Rosemary passed hers to Peter. "Go down to the kitchen and wait there."

"Rosemary, what —"

"I'll catch you up." She waited as Peter clopped carefully down the stairs, then she eased herself to Faith's door and turned the knob.

Faith was in bed, covers pulled around her, arms draped across the bedspread. She breathed deeply, and didn't quite snore.

Rosemary tiptoed to her side and set an envelope on the bedside table. She paused and smiled down at Faith in her sleep.

"Good luck in your studies, Dr. Watson," she said, and she leaned over and kissed Faith's cheek.

Faith murmured, and rolled onto her side.

~~ :•: ~~

Holding candles, Rosemary and Peter clopped down the basement steps. The place was clear of crates and full of scuffed footprints. Faith had thrown up her hands and left it undisturbed.

"Are you sure this isn't a wild goose chase?" asked Peter.

"If it is, then I'm sorry," said Rosemary. "But we have to try. I had a dream."

"That's inspiring."

The trap door had been locked with a simple wedge of wood and an admonition from a police officer not to touch it until the construction crew came to seal it up. Rosemary pried out the wedge and lifted the door. She shone the candle down the steps. "There's a boat down there. The police must have left it after they cleared the basement."

"You can't be serious," said Peter.

Rosemary took his hand. "Come on."

They climbed down the stairs to the boat, lit the lanterns, and untied the boat from the jetty. Peter took up the pole while Rosemary guided the rudder. They floated forward in silence.

"The portals have all closed," said Peter. "You said so. So where are we going?"

Rosemary shrugged. "I said the portals were flowing downstream as the river died. We forgot: there's one last place for a portal to exist. And after all the weird things that have happened to us, I'm giving this a shot."

They slipped further downstream. The tunnel widened. All the passing branches were dark.

Peter dipped his pole into the water. "You know, if we make it back, we'll have been gone four whole months."

"I know."

"We'll have missed a term of school, not to mention our scholarships."

"We'll just have to reapply."

"And explain our four-month absence?"

"I know," said Rosemary. "We'll have a lot of catching up to do." She chuckled. "It's almost easier just to stay here."

They drifted on silently in the dark.

"Well," said Peter. "There is hot, running water to look forward to."

Rosemary grinned. "And central heating."

"And television."

"And the Internet."

"And your science degree," said Peter. "And your career."

"And our friends," said Rosemary. "And our family."

He frowned down at her. "What are we going to tell everyone?"

"I don't know."

"What are we going to tell your parents?"

"The truth."

"The whole truth?"

"Yes."

They floated further in silence. After a long while, they rounded a curve and came out into Aldous Birge's ruined port. They passed the broken jetties, the gouged walls where the gaslights used to be, and the scorched and blackened bricks. The door to the warehouse was bricked over.

Rosemary tugged at Peter's sleeve. She pointed.

At the mouth of the underground river, where the tunnel gave way to open sky, a boat passed across the horizon. Its rigging was lit up like a Christmas tree. It let out a belt of its horn. The image faded and flickered before resuming, strong as before.

"The last portal," said Rosemary. "At the mouth of the river."

Peter drew a shaky breath as he pushed toward the portal. Rosemary looked up at him. "You scared?"

He laughed. "Can you believe it? Yeah. I can't think why."

"We have a lot of questions to answer, a lot of things to do, and a lot of decisions to make," said Rosemary.

"I was all set on being a construction worker," said Peter. "Now I have to decide whether to go back to journalism school. But I can't go to London; that would be too far from you. It's all too much, too soon."

"Peter?"

He looked at her. She let go of the rudder and stood up. The boat coasted. "Whatever happens, whatever we face, if the last few months have taught me anything, it's this." She reached up and kissed him. "We'll face it together."

"I love you, Rosemary."

"I love you too." Then she sat back down and grabbed the rudder. "Now." She pointed. "Forward!"

Peter pushed the pole, and the boat slipped forward and vanished into the future.

AUTHOR'S NOTE

~~ :•: ~~

I spent most of my childhood years growing up in Toronto living in a townhouse on McCaul Street. The street was on the edge of the downtown core, with the fronts of its houses staring east at the rising towers of the hospital district and the Ontario Hydro headquarters. It is an old residential street being transformed by the city's expanding core. Our townhouse, we believe, was originally built in the 1890s on a site that was once cricket grounds, but more significantly, before that, a peculiar old creek bed.

Two blocks from my house is a short stub of a street, mostly a delivery lane for the University of Toronto, known as Taddle Creek Road. This street is one of the few reminders of a significant river that used to flow through Toronto's downtown core. Taddle Creek started life in the neighbourhood of Wychwood near the Bathurst/Davenport intersection and meandered southeast through the university grounds, possibly even beneath our house, before reaching Lake Ontario near where the St. Lawrence Market is today.

By all accounts, the creek was a treasure. The University of Toronto was originally built with prime views of the creek and its associated wetlands, but encroaching development polluted the Taddle, and gradually the City of Toronto built over it, transforming the creek into a series of bricked-up storm sewers. The stretch through the university grounds, a great portion of which is known as Philosopher's Walk, was the last to be covered over in 1884.

There is a mystique about this buried river. Garrison Creek was longer, and still has a greater impact on the city's topology, but Taddle seems to capture the imagination, much like the Fleet in London, England. Perhaps because of its downtown course, the Taddle is a symbol of both the folly and might of industrial progress. For locals, we remembered the Taddle with a strange pride: here was a river we built over. Here was a great watercourse that we killed. Urban legends built up around the Taddle. I was told that there were caverns associated with the buried river beneath Queen's Park. I was told that the University subway line made use of these caverns during construction. Most of these tales are probably apocryphal, but they are a part of my identification with this river.

And at the back basement of our house on McCaul Street, there was a small hole in the concrete foundation, and a strange patch of floor that sounded a little hollow. We had no idea what this was. Could it have been a secret chamber that was used when the house was owned by bootleggers during the 1920s and '30s? (My father has a pretty good idea that the house was used as such during Prohibition because, during his childhood in the '50s, after his father had bought it, it was amazing how many drunks showed up at the door at the middle of the night asking for a bottle). Or was it one of the caverns associated with the Taddle?

Of course, it was probably nothing. But the idea that there was something under my place stayed with me in the years after we moved to Kitchener. And as I tackled the tale of Peter and Rosemary at eighteen, these elements decided to make their contribution. What if Peter and Rosemary, helping Theo move into that basement apartment, fell through that floor, fell into the Taddle, and walked through the storm drains back into time, emerging on the university grounds in 1884, just as the Taddle was being buried?

My story probably takes several artistic licences. The size and shape of the storm sewer tunnels in this book are probably larger than what reality calls for (although given that some people have little difficulty in exploring the storm drains of Toronto, perhaps I'm not that far off). And the cavern Peter and Rosemary fall into probably doesn't exist. But it's still a part of the city's collective imagination. And I hope that this lends my

story the validity it needs. This is a fantasy, after all —
an urban fantasy. And if I can't take some liberties with
reality to tell a fantastical story about my childhood city,
what's the point of being an author?

Today, the Taddle is remembered in plaques and in
flooded basements. There has been talk about exhuming
the water course, though it seems unlikely given the cost.
But various groups are coming together to remember
the many rivers that Toronto has buried.

HAVE YOU READ ALL
THE UNWRITTEN BOOKS?

Take a step back in the series and check out other books by James Bow

Fathom Five
978-1-55002-692-4
$12.99, £6.99

On the surface, Peter McAllister has a good life: a good school, good friends, good times — even if his best friend is a girl, sort of a geek, and maybe even more than a friend. But it's been years since the death of his parents landed him in this small town and he still feels as if his life in Clarksbury is just an inch deep. Does he really belong? Only Rosemary seems real. Then a mysterious woman named Fiona appears who tells him he's a changeling — a fairy child left to live in the human world — and that it's time to come home. Can Rosemary convince him that Fiona is lying? Or is it possible that Fiona is telling the truth?

The Unwritten Girl
978-1-55002-604-7
$12.99, £6.99

Years ago Rosemary Watson's brother, Theo, suffered a nervous breakdown, and Rosemary, now entering junior high, is constantly teased about it. She tries to hide in books, but even there she's uneasy: she can't stand to see characters suffer. Rosemary and Peter — the new kid in school with issues of his own — are thrown together and soon find themselves on a life-or-death quest to rescue Rosemary's brother, who has lost himself in a book. With the help of Peter and her guide, fairy shape-shifter Puck, Rosemary must face the storybook perils of the Land of Fiction and learn to open her heart before it is too late.

Available at your favourite bookseller.

DUNDURN PRESS
www.dundurn.com

Tell us your story! What did you think of this book?
Join the conversation at
www.definingcanada.ca/tell-your-story
by telling us what you think.